WELCOME TO WESPIRTECH

SHORT FICTION FROM THE ENTANGLED UNIVERSE

MARY E. LOWD

For Cuyla, Kacie, and Kyle

Having dinner with the three of you on the weekends, drinking tea, chatting, playing Magic together, watching you play Sega, sharing movies and conversation—that was the highlight of my high school years. So many of the things I still love are things you introduced into my life.

Thank you

CONTENTS

PREFACE

If someone wanted to be charitable, they could say I was a loner in high school. This is the kind way to say that I didn't really have friends. One of my best friends—more of a family friend, who may or may not have returned my strong sense of attachment—was several years older than me. She graduated before I did, and she went away to college. But she came home to visit, and when she did, we all sat around her family's kitchen table—her family and mine—having tea while she told us stories about her new adventures in a magical land called Caltech. We watched the movie *Real Genius*, and she pointed out everything in that fantastical 80s romp that was based on something real in the place she actually lived now. She had found a place where she belonged. A wild, wacky, crazy, fun, complicated place full of painfully smart people. I wanted nothing more than to follow in her footsteps.

I didn't get into Caltech, but I did get into a different high-level tech college, Harvey Mudd. My experience there was... not good. But I learned a lot. Not necessarily a lot of science—I ended up majoring in English through Pomona, a neighboring college—but a lot about scientists and what they're like when they're all crammed together into crowded dorms, isolated away from the outside world, and put under a great deal of pressure.

I always wanted to be a science-fiction writer, since long before I learned about Caltech. I had wanted to study physics at a tech college so that when I wrote about physics, I would get it right. Instead, I ended up studying physicists—and biologists, engineers, chemists, and mathematicians—and the ways they interacted with each other and their world. So, after I managed to scrape together a Bachelors of Science in English degree from my off-brand Caltech, I immediately set to work. I invented Wespirtech, and I poured everything I had learned during college into that magical place. My version of Caltech, except far away among the stars.

The first story I wrote was "The Genetic Menagerie," but I have continued writing about Wespirtech, off and on, for twenty years since then. The stories in this collection reflect facets of that grand, strange, and sometimes quite broken institution. The atmo-domes of Wespirtech hold the magic I always imagined at Caltech, but also the struggles and dysfunction I encountered for real at Harvey Mudd.

Science is one of the most important things we have. Studying the real world and trying to discover how it actually works is a truly noble calling. But scientists are people, and people make mistakes, foolish choices, and mess everything up with their feelings and relationships. I've tried to capture some of that, mixed in with the wacky, far-future antics of scientists who have access to technologies we don't have yet.

In the end, a tech college was not a place I belonged, so I created my own place. You're welcome to join me there.

NOTE ON THE 2ND EDITION

This book was originally released in 2014 before I had really finished writing it. My first two novels—*Otters In Space* and *Otters In Space 2: Jupiter, Deadly*—had recently been picked up by a small publisher, FurPlanet, and I wanted to sell copies at local events. However, a table with only two books on it is a sad affair. So, I took all the short stories I'd written at the time and managed to put together three meagre collections—*Welcome to Wespirtech*, *Beyond Wespirtech*, and *The Opposite of Memory*—which I self-published. For the next nine years, I pursued traditional publishing, and my self-published collections fell to the side. But now that I'm in my forties and tired of the nonsense inherent to the publishing industry, I've returned to my roots, and it was time to make this book what it was always meant to be.

Two of the most important stories in this book—stories that really pull the rest of them together—were written after the first edition was released, and one of those stories is wholly original to this edition, never published before.

I never stopped loving this book, even when it was incomplete. Now that I see what it's become, I love it even more. I hope, dear reader, you will love it too.

1

BREATHING THE AIR AT WESPIRTECH

The girl was science; chemistry personified, manifested in a physical form. This is not to say that the other scientists of Wespirtech were lining up in a snaky queue through the Daedalus Complex halls to see her, study her, consult with her like she was some sort of oracle. At least, Keida didn't think so. Her new roommate, Rhiannon, was too quiet, and serious, to draw that kind of attention.

No, it meant Keida could see chemistry thoughts as they formed in Rhiannon's brain. The evidence was perfectly clear on her face; a look that bespoke particles and molecules moving, joining, breaking apart and reforming in an abstract space she saw, approximately five inches above her own head. Keida was afraid to interrupt. A single word from her might break the spell. All those invisible molecules would dissipate and undo hours of silent work.

So, Rhiannon's chemistry thoughts functioned like a shield, and she brandished them as such. As long as she focused on her research, she lived in a chemistry-land only she could see. Rhiannon had been hiding there since Keida first arrived. It was a withdrawal, a postponement of the inevitable.

There is only so long two girls can room together in silence. Eventually, one of them has to speak.

Perhaps it wouldn't have taken them as long if they'd had to introduce themselves. However, the Hoilyn worker who helped Keida bring her luggage from the shuttle facilitated that. It was a long walk from the shuttle port to the dormitories, even though it was entirely indoors. Every building in Wespirtech, except the very newest, was connected through the network of underground hallways known as the Daedalus Complex. That's the sign of architecture on a world without atmosphere.

When they had arrived at her new room, Keida saw there were two beds and asked, "I have a roommate?"

"Yes. Two girls, one room," the Hoilyn answered. He bobbed his knobbly head in imitation of a human nod. The gesture had been strangely disfigured by the sinuous length of his furry neck.

Keida began pulling her luggage into the fastidiously neat, obviously unoccupied half of the room. Keida's half. She set her daypack on the perfectly-made bed; Keida suspected her bed would never be made so neatly again. She had a tendency towards sloppiness. The Hoilyn stacked her larger suitcases next to the closet.

As he was leaving, Keida stopped her helper to ask, "Do you know my roommate? Is she... nice?"

He answered in his broken, ghetto Solanese: "Yes, Rhiannon. Good girl. Good quiet. Dark hair." He fluttered his clunky hands, covered by keratinous calluses, by the side of his head. Keida wouldn't have understood his pantomime of Rhiannon's thick, wavy, brown hair if Rhiannon herself hadn't timidly appeared at the door. Her own door. And, yet, since it was no longer completely her own, she felt reluctant to enter the room. Rhiannon was shy.

"This her!" the Hoilyn exclaimed, putting his arm behind

Rhiannon to urge her in. "Rhia-nnon," he said, "meet room-mate. Keida. Also good girl. Two good girls."

He left them together to get acquainted, but after a few shy smiles, Keida lost herself in unpacking, and Rhiannon made her escape to chemistry-land.

Rhiannon might have stayed lost in her research, among the simple interactions of algae DNA, gamma radiation, and artificial proteins indefinitely. People are much more complicated. However, the gawkily tall, straight-haired girl, who now came in and out of her room at will, strangely fascinated her.

After several days, the days of Keida's orientation to the Wespirtech research facilities, Rhiannon felt a pressure building to speak. Of course, by then, Keida had given up on speaking to Rhiannon. Keida had run the gauntlet of the official Wespirtech orientation. With the other initiates, she'd been led on tours of all the labs, shown previews of the most cutting edge research, and trained in the computer and security systems. The message had been clear: research at Wespirtech is groundbreaking and exciting. The more Keida had learned about Wespirtech, the more her mysterious, serious roommate intimidated her. Rhiannon would find no reprieve there. If the two girls were to talk, Rhiannon would have to open the discussion.

She leaned her head forward and her thick brown hair fell like a wall between her and the world. Keida couldn't see that the chemistry thoughts were gone, but she sensed a change in Rhiannon's posture.

"My first-year roommate barely talked to me," Rhiannon said, her voice oddly monotonal, like she was struggling to make herself say the words, to say any words at all. "I was hoping she'd be my friend. You need a friend when you come to a new place, but she was too busy. I want to do better."

Even though Rhiannon had utterly ignored Keida for days on end, the new girl ardently admired her and instantly forgave the transgression. She saw, in Rhiannon, everything she'd imagined a Wespirtech researcher to be. Everything she wanted to be. "Then let's be friends," Keida said, as if declaring the intention were enough to make it so.

Face obscured by her wavy wall of dark, frizzy hair, Rhiannon smiled. "I'd like that."

And so a friendship began, because both girls were young and simple enough when it came to human interaction to believe that friendship can be as simple as that. And maybe it is, sometimes, for some people, in some situations. But sometimes, the world or your backgrounds or your different lives get in the way, and a shared intention—brief and flickering—is not enough.

Keida and Rhiannon soon found their areas of study overlapped. A natural synergy emerged between Rhiannon's abstract chemistry and Keida's hands-on biology. Together, they worked more than twice as fast, ideas bouncing between them as rapidly as molecules in one of their experiments subjected to gamma radiation. DNA mutated and evolved in the petri dishes they filled with algae samples as quickly as their conversation could flow from one topic to the next, morphing from serious scientific inquiry to giggling in-jokes and Wespirtech gossip and back again, looping endlessly and barely stopping long enough for the two girls to sleep.

Soon they had designed an entirely new species of algae, perfectly suited to grow and live and respirate eternally inside enclosed packages. Self-contained ecosystems that could be abandoned and ignored in storage chambers for decades without degrading, but when fed carbon-dioxide and an absolutely minimal amount of light-energy, they returned almost entirely purified oxygen. Not quite pure, but almost. The impurities, though—they smelled almost sweet, almost like perfume. Subtle, nearly unnoticeable.

Keida and Rhiannon's algae packs would revolutionize

space travel. The Wespirtech administrators—who live for experiments that have practical applications that can actually make money—were ecstatic and assured Rhiannon and her new partner in science that the algae packs would replace the old, standard models in every spaceship, atmo-dome, and space station within the Human Expansion in a matter of years, expanding outward, beginning with Wespirtech. A factory on another moon orbiting planet Da Vinci put the algae packs into immediate production, and both Keida and Rhiannon were given expanded budgets for their future studies, nearly free-reign in choosing their next projects.

THE DAY the new algae packs replaced the old standards on Wespirtech was deemed a holiday, and the administrators paid all the Hoilyn workers to put on a grand celebration for the scientists—decorations, feasts, and entertainment, all hosted inside one of the biology department's more park-like atmo-domes, surrounded by the overgrown ferns and fruit trees that were all experiments in their own right.

Keida walked along the pathways in the atmo-dome between the burgeoning trees, heavy with their gengineered fruits, in a daze, amazed by the sights, sounds, and smells. In one cul-de-sac among the trees, a Hoilyn band played music on instruments that seemed to have been carved from giant shells, combining low, sustained booms with sparkly higher notes in a hypnotic synthesis. Another Hoilyn juggled little fuzzy animals who squeaked delightedly—at least, they seemed delighted— at the apex of every throw, as if they considered the whole ordeal to be some kind of tiny carnival ride. Even more Hoilyn danced in synchrony, wearing flowing robes and scarves tied around their long necks with weighted balls at their ends; the weighted scarves, filmy and gauzy, swung hypnotically as the

Hoilyn swayed their necks back and forth in rhythm with the haunting music.

The food was even more exciting—strange dishes unlike anything Keida had ever tried before. Keida asked the Hoilyn servers about each one and learned they were all native dishes. "Native to where?" Keida asked.

"Why here," the Hoilyn server who had just filled Keida's plate with a second serving of a rich, red stew-like dish answered. She gestured with her keratinous hoof-like hand.

"This moon?" Keida asked, surprised. The moon around Wespirtech was a desolate rock. Nothing could live here. Not the Hoilyn, not the fuzzy creatures being juggled, and not whatever had lived in those beautiful, pearlescent shells before they'd been hollowed out to become instruments. Certainly not any of the spongy, rubbery, delicious textures in the stew Keida was holding. Whether plant or beast, they all had to have come from elsewhere.

"No, no, silly!" The Hoilyn laughed, a hearty, throaty sound, and gestured again. This time, Keida followed the gesture more carefully and realized the Hoilyn was pointing—as much as she could with a hand holding a ladle full of stew—at the planet Wespirtech's moon was orbiting. The planet Da Vinci.

"I didn't know there was intelligent life on Da Vinci before humans came here," Keida said.

"Long time," the Hoilyn answered. "Long civilization."

"Did you get to the moon on your own?" Keida pressed, suddenly curious.

The Hoilyn woman shook her head, causing her long neck to sway like a sine wave. It was an unnatural gesture on a being with a neck so long, clearly something the Hoilyn had picked up from the humans employing them. Keida wondered what kind of gestures the Hoilyn used among themselves. She wondered for the first time what their native language sounded like. What their society had been like before humans came.

The Hoilyn were such an indispensable part of Wespirtech, doing so much of the grunt work that allowed all the scientists to keep daydreaming and studying and experimenting without worrying about practical matters like feeding themselves or cleaning, that it was hard to imagine Wespirtech without them. Or for that matter, them without Wespirtech. But today, seeing how much of the celebration for the new algae packs came from their culture, it was clear to Keida for the first time that the Hoilyn very much existed separately from Wespirtech. She swore to herself that going forward, she would learn more about them.

"You're here!" Rhiannon's voice chimed from behind Keida.

When Keida whirled around, careful not to spill her stew, she found the smaller woman standing close, her bushy hair pulled back in a ponytail for once, leaving only a few dark strands of curls loose around her ears and forehead. "Of course," Keida said. "I've been wandering around. Seeing the sights."

"Oh, the celebration?" Rhiannon asked. She waved a hand dismissively. "They're all like this. Every time we celebrate something. It's fun, but you get used to it."

Keida couldn't imagine dismissing the Hoilyn celebration so easily, but then, she hadn't been at Wespirtech for long. There were still wonders to discover. Everything at Wespirtech was a wonder.

"Come on!" Rhiannon entreated, grabbing Keida by her free hand and pulling her away from the row of food carts. Her hand was cool and small, and Keida followed along docilely, feeling overly tall and awkward as Rhiannon, with her smaller stature, pulled her between various groups of other scientists, standing around, chatting, snacking, and generally enjoying the festivities. Rhiannon could duck through places easily where Keida struggled to fit.

When she got a chance, Keida ditched her bowl of stew on

the corner of one of the tables that had been set up for the party as they passed it. Either she'd make her way back to it after whatever Rhiannon was pulling her toward, or the Hoilyn would get it when they cleaned up. She hoped leftovers from the party would be part of the dining hall offerings tomorrow. She really liked that red stew.

Keida and Rhiannon arrived at the edge of the atmo-dome, beside the open hatch in the floor that led to stair descending into the underground Daedelus Complex and the airlock in the dome's outer wall that led to the inhospitable, atmosphere-less world outside. The airlock itself was built from gleaming metal, but the dome around it was all clear, letting Keida see through to the desolate gray rocky landscape outside.

The rocky gray horizon with the night sky above, unpolluted by anything as gauche as an atmosphere blurring the sunlight into cloudy colors, was beautiful in a stark, minimalist kind of way. Not like the dancing Hoilyn with their colorful scarves surrounded by trees whose branches were weighed down by gemlike fruit that grew too large for the poor branches to support it. Inside the dome was life, so much life, almost too much. Outside, nothing but dust and stone.

Several administrators, marked by their uniforms, stood beside the airlock. None of the scientists could be controlled well enough to make them wear uniforms; they wore what they liked, whatever made them comfortable, and as long as they kept producing science—ideally science that could be packaged up and converted into money—the administrators didn't care.

Rhiannon rocked forward on her toes, making her briefly taller, and said, "I brought her!" to the group of administrators.

Keida recognized most of them—Wespirtech is a small place, and even scientists with their heads in the clouds (metaphorical clouds, of course, given the moon's lack of atmosphere) eventually became aware of the non-scientists around them who also lived in the halls of the Daedelus Complex and also ate in the dining halls. Though, Keida was more tuned into the other people of all species around her than most of the other scientists were. It had taken Rhiannon years to remember the names of any of the administrators who allocated her funding and laboratory space, regardless of how much of her life depended on them and their choices.

"One of the administrators stepped forward and said, "Wonderful. We thought the two of you should have the honor of installing the first algae packs at the institute. The rest of them, of course, will be installed by technicians. But this is the first!"

Keida and Rhiannon exchanged a look that mixed excitement with awkwardness and uncertainty. The administrator held out one of their algae packs—it didn't look quite the same as the prototypes they'd whipped up with the help of some of the local Wespirtech engineers. Those had been droopy and duct-taped together. This pack was sleek and taut; the translucent exterior showed the bright green algae almost glowing in the quasi-crystalline matrix of the colloidal rendering on the inside, rich with all the nutrients the algae needed to stay healthy for decades and decades.

Keida and Rhiannon both reached toward the proffered pack at the same time, and their fingers bumped together, causing them both to laugh. "You take it," Rhiannon said. "I'm just the theoretician. You actually built it. You should install it."

"Okay," Keida said, unsure of herself. She felt weird about Rhiannon downplaying her role in their creation like that—they'd been equal partners, equal creators, and everything Keida had done guiding the algae to grow differently would have been meaningless without the principles behind Rhiannon's ideas guiding her. But she couldn't think fast enough—certainly not with all those administrators staring at her, expecting things from her—to figure out exactly what was wrong with Rhiannon's words or how to object to them gracefully. So, she simply took the algae pack.

The bright green packet felt squishy in her hands—firm on the outside, but uneven, movable, and slidey underneath. Like it would slip out of her hands if she let it. She held on tight and watched carefully as the administrator explained where the pack would slot into the air filtration system on the wall beside the airlock. Under the administrator's guidance, Rhiannon reached in with her smaller, doll-like hands and took out the old algae pack. The algae inside it was a dull, evergreen shade compared to the almost neon, peridot green of the new pack.

Once the slot was empty, Keida placed the new pack inside, and it locked easily into place, as if it had been made exactly for that spot. Keida supposed it had been. Though, she hadn't been involved in that part of the engineering. Once she and Rhiannon had proved the prototype worked beyond their wild imaginings, the whole project had been taken off their hands. Which they hadn't minded. They'd finished with the fun part already.

The administrators, standing in an overbearing semi-circle around the two scientists, applauded politely as the new algae pack came online and began filtering the atmo-dome's air with a quiet hiss. Not knowing quite how to react, Keida dipped her head in a quasi-bow, and Rhiannon smiled shyly, letting her wall of hair fall forward to hide the sides of her face. She must have pulled out the band that held it back in a ponytail when Keida wasn't paying attention.

"Congratulations to the both of you!" one of the administrators said. Another added, "We're excited to learn about your next projects!" Accolades continued, vague but warm, until both scientists were quietly uncomfortable and very glad to be set free, back to the celebration.

"What do you think you'll work on next?" Keida asked Rhiannon as the two of them wandered along the tree-lined paths of the atmo-dome, vaguely heading back to where Keida had ditched her bowl of stew. It had already been cleared away when they got back to the tables, but the food carts were still out, the Hoilyn working them were still serving food, so Keida got herself another bowl.

All the while, Rhiannon followed along, seemingly oblivious to the excitement around them, telling Keida about her ideas for upcoming projects. They were all far too abstract and exacting to interest Keida. She liked to work with things she could get her hands on—plants, animals. Things that grow and change.

Algae had been somewhat outside Keida's comfort zone— too small, too few cells, no organ systems at all—but she admired Rhiannon so much and had been so excited to work with her. Keida was disappointed, listening to Rhiannon's excitement over upcoming projects that had no room for her, to realize their collaboration was truly over. They were still friends and roommates, of course, but Rhiannon's chemistry and Keida's biology research would take them in different directions going forward. It had been a one-time collaboration, a liminal space, already over. Keida hoped it wouldn't hurt their friendship, no longer focusing together on a shared professional passion.

Keida felt a little lost, like she had when she'd first arrived at Wespirtech. She spent the rest of the celebration day trying to make new friends. She didn't want to feel so wholly dependent on her friendship with Rhiannon to feel like she belonged, like she had a place here. She needed to carve out a space for herself as an individual. She meant no disrespect to her friendship with Rhiannon and in no way meant to put extra distance between the two of them. In fact, Keida hoped that by building more friendships, it would take the pressure off her friendship with her roommate, making it possible for them to stay close, making it less likely that any sense of professional aimlessness she felt would interfere with how she and Rhiannon felt about each other...

However, Rhiannon didn't know what was going on inside Keida's head. Arguably, Keida didn't either—she just felt a pressure inside her, pushing her toward other people, pressing her into making new connections with other Wespirtech scientists. So, ironically, Keida's instinctive, subconscious desire to protect her friendship with Rhiannon led to her creating the exact distance she feared.

All Rhiannon saw was Keida drifting away from her, spending more time on other people, being more social than she knew, herself, how to be. Rhiannon wasn't just quiet or introverted; she was painfully shy. She'd been at Wespirtech for several years before Keida arrived, without making any significant friendships, only passing acquaintances with the people around her. If she'd known how some of the other scientists saw her—focused, driven, intimidating—she might have been less afraid to reach out to them and form friendships of her own. As it was, Rhiannon had trouble seeing anything coherent in the chaotic complexity of human interaction. Humans don't move as simply and predictably as atoms and molecules. And Rhiannon found it easier to withdraw, once again, into the chemistry-land inside her own mind, surrounded by equations simple enough to solve, riddles with correct answers.

OVER THE YEARS THAT FOLLOWED, Keida's career soared. She rarely collaborated with other scientists anymore, preferring to keep her work and her friendships separate, at least as much as was possible while living in a science institute on a desolate moon. During the days, she perfected the DNA of designer creatures that thrilled the administrators with their usefulness and practical applications. At night, she moved easily from one social group to the next, participating in the joys of living in a place where her compatriots sizzled with so much brilliance that the whole place practically effervesced. The games, the parties, the dramatic on-again-off-again love affairs—Keida participated in them all. But also, she let them flow over her. She took part in them, but they didn't really become a part of her. Her heart lay elsewhere.

Every few days, Keida slipped away from the hallways of the Daedelus Complex to the older, more rundown section of Wespirtech that the Hoilyn workers lived in.

The very first Wespirtech building had been a big, rectangular affair, not very exciting to look at, simply jutting up in the middle of the dusty gray horizon on the desolate moon. Since then, a couple other buildings had sprouted up, and the underground tunnels of the Daedelus Complex had burrowed beneath, connecting the different buildings. Then eventually, as Wespirtech had become more and more successful, atmo-domes had been added, allowing arboretums to be filled with gengineered plants worked on by the biologists.

Most of Wespirtech was dingy and gray, not very aesthetically pleasing, but Keida spent enough time working in the arboretums that the dreariness of the scenery didn't get her down. And whatever the first building—the Millicent G. Lum building, named for Wespirtech's founder—lacked in visual appeal on the outside or in architectural design, the Hoilyn who lived there had made up for with colorful, beautiful hangings and intricate sculptures everywhere inside. The parts of Wespirtech inhabited by the actual scientists might be decorated approximately like college dorm rooms, plastered with cheap posters and whiteboards covered in scribblings, but inside the Millicent G. Lum building, it was an entirely different world.

The air always smelled liked festival days there, filled with spices and the rich, complex aromas of stews and roasts that slow-cooked for days before they were ready. Laughter and singing and haunting, sparkly music floated through the halls. The Hoilyn were welcoming to Keida, and by spending time among them, volunteering to help with whatever they were willing to let her help with, she learned how to cook the red stew she'd loved so much, learned how to play a few of the instruments carved from pearlescent shells, and developed a halting, sometimes laughable, but almost fluent grasp of their language.

When Keida didn't feel like she quite belonged at Wespirtech, she at least felt welcomed by the Hoilyn.

Then the worst thing happened. Well, the worst thing for Keida. For the Hoilyn, it was that complicated, mixed blessing: a diagnosis.

When you're already suffering from a mysterious illness, sometimes, just getting a label that explains what it is, why it's happening, and outlines what—if anything—you can do about it feels like a miracle.

After years of confusion and sickness, a recurring illness among the Hoilyn workers was linked to the impurities— almost imperceptible, sweet-smelling like perfume—released by Keida and Rhiannon's state-of-the-art algae packs.

The same algae packs that had infiltrated outward, being installed in every spaceship, atmo-dome, and space station in the Human Expansion. Ever since the first day when Keida and Rhiannon had together installed the shiny new algae pack they'd designed in one of Wespirtech's atmo-domes, the overall health of the Hoilyn workers had been falling. Respiratory diffi- culties. Headaches. Unexplained nausea. That very first day, once the algae packs had been installed in the Millicent G. Lum building, a Hoilyn child had gone into anaphylactic shock and nearly died. Incidences like that had only increased over the following years.

And Keida had had no idea about any of it. Sure, she'd

spent time among the Hoilyn, and sure, sometimes people she knew had struggled or fallen sick, but she didn't have the historical context to realize how much worse their health struggles had become overnight. Or had she? Should she have connected the dots?

Keida didn't know, and it tore her up inside. There's no way to apologize for making a mistake like that. She was a research biologist, but she wasn't a doctor. She hadn't been privy to the exact, intimate details of the plague she'd brought upon the Hoilyn. She wasn't the one to discover the connection.

As soon as Keida learned about the effects of her and Rhiannon's invention though, she went to the administrators, meeting with one after another, arguing and pleading, trying to convince them to replace the new algae packs with the old ones.

None of the administrators would listen. It was like arguing with a cash register. They'd say, "We don't have the budget for that. Replacing all the algae packs would be a huge expense and interfere with our mission to advance applied science." All Keida heard was, "But that would cost us money."

Some of the administrators even tried to argue that the money saved by using Keida and Rhiannon's algae packs had saved lives, enough lives to make up for any cost to the Hoilyn workers' health. That was a kind of math Keida felt extremely uncomfortable doing, and yet, she couldn't entirely refute the possibility. Fresh air is the difference between life and death on a space station.

Besides, the administrators argued, the Hoilyn were a minor species who only lived on the planet below—planet Da Vinci which they had called Hoilour before humans had come and renamed it—and nowhere else in the galaxy. So far. And now, unless something changed, they never would. And it was Keida's fault.

In the end, no matter how much Keida argued, the administrators left Wespirtech's Hoilyn workers with a simple choice: they could continue working through their growing infirmities or they were welcome to return to the planet below and breathe its bountiful fresh air if they no longer liked the air at Wespirtech. If they could prove their health had declined since the new algae packs were installed—which of course the administrators made very difficult, dependent on comparative health records from both before and after the installation— they were afforded a modest relocation fee. Very few Hoilyn were ultimately able to claim it, and even among those, it was unclear as to whether they actually ever received the money.

The Hoilyn population at Wespirtech dwindled. Keida hoped for a brief, shining moment that the science institute would find itself in a state of neglect—trash cans overflowing, food spoiling, dust collecting everywhere—and that everything would grind to a halt until the old algae filters were reinstated and the Hoily could return. Of course, that didn't happen. The engineers of Wespirtech had designed far too many extremely useful robots for that to happen.

One by one, the Hoilyn moved away, and job by job, they were quietly replaced by robots who did mechanically perfect jobs of cleaning, uninspired but functional jobs of cooking, and left a giant gaping hole that filled Keida's heart and vision. Everywhere at Wespirtech, all she could see was what was now missing. She thought, for sure, the first time a festival day happened, the other scientists would miss the Hoilyn too. Their cooking. Their music. Their dancing. Their juggling. Their culture. And maybe some did. But others complimented the new style of celebration with stereos blasting recordings of the same music they already liked, extravagant foods shipped up from Da Vinci and reheated rather than slow-cooked in their own halls, and mechanically perfect but strangely soul-less choreographed dancing from sub-sentient robots designed especially to dance.

Heartbroken, Keida left the festival in the parklike atmo-dome. It had been a celebration of one of her colleagues, another biologist who had invented some kind of device that let you hook your brain up to that of an animal and experience the animal's feelings. It sounded cool. Everything at Wespirtech was almost impossibly cool.

Keida didn't want cool anymore. She wanted the warmth of the Hoilyn back. Instinctively, she wandered the halls of the Daedelus Complex until she found herself staring at Rhiannon's door.

Rhiannon still lived in the same room they'd shared, way back when, years ago. They hadn't been roommates in ages. Both of them had reached the levels of success that administrators liked to reward and encourage, and one of the most standard rewards was a private room.

Keida thought back on the times when she and Rhiannon had stayed up all night in that room—the room right in front of her—talking and scheming and brainstorming and planning. Part of her missed those days, and most of her remembered how young and scared and uncertain she'd felt. She'd felt like she needed to prove herself.

But look where proving herself had gotten her.

Keida shook her head, and she almost walked away without knocking at the door. But somehow, Rhiannon must have heard her in the hall, because her old roommate opened the door, saw Keida standing there, cocked her head and gestured for her to come in.

THE TWO WOMEN sat side by side on Rhiannon's perfectly made bed. The room didn't have two beds anymore. The second bed had been replaced with a desk. It was covered with notes and chemical models, an open laptop, and a couple of beakers of brightly colored liquids. Keida wasn't sure whether those were decorative, beverages, or experiments. She didn't ask.

Once again, the two women—who had been mere girls when they'd met—sat in silence. Once again, it fell to Rhiannon to break the silence.

"I thought you'd be at the party," she said.

"I was," Keida answered. She felt like she owed Rhiannon more words than that, after appearing so randomly at her door, but those were the only words that came to mind.

"I know you like the festival days." Rhiannon smiled, weakly. She felt that she'd lost Keida to the chaos of Wespirtech's social scene years ago. Even among scientists—all odd and socially awkward—Rhiannon still didn't feel like she fit in, and she'd watched Keida with awe, envy, and more than a little sadness over the years. They'd always stayed friends... ostensibly. But they'd never been close again, not like they'd been during those early days.

"It's not the same without the Hoilyn," Keida said. She lay back on the bed and stared up at the ceiling. Rhiannon had decorated it with glowing stars since she'd moved out, moved to her own room. She liked the stars. They weren't glowing right now, but she could imagine how pretty they'd look when the lights were turned off.

"The robots don't put on as good of a festival?" Rhiannon wasn't sure what they were talking about. She wasn't sure what had brought Keida here. She was excited to be receiving Keida's attention, but she knew that such attention could be fleeting. She didn't know what had brought it on, and she didn't know what would end it.

"It's not about the robots," Keida said, placing her hands over her face. "It's about the Hoilyn." She drew a deep breath, pulled her hands down her face, and then sat up again. She looked at Rhiannon, frowning, brow crinkling. "Don't you feel guilty? About what happened with them? About our part in it?"

Rhiannon's brow crinkled and mouth turned down in a frown, unconsciously mirroring Keida's expression. She felt like shrugging. She knew that Keida had spent a lot of time with the Hoilyn; she knew about Keida's arguments with the administrators, trying to undo the work they'd done together. But she didn't understand. Even so, she knew better than to shrug. She said, "We didn't know. And our algae packs have done a lot of good."

Keida sighed, frustrated that Rhiannon was defending their work, just the same as the administrators had. Rhiannon was frustrated that Keida would devalue it—because for all the damage done to the Hoilyn, the administrators weren't wrong about the good their algae packs had done. They weren't factually wrong. But did that make them right?

"You don't understand," Keida insisted, stumbling right onto the exact words Rhiannon had been thinking. Because she agreed—she did not understand. "They can't breathe here. Not reliably. The air just stops working for them, and sits in their lungs like a dead weight while they gasp uselessly at it. I've seen it happen, for years! I just didn't know it was because of something I was responsible for... something we did. Not at first."

"Of course not," Rhiannon reassured Keida. "How could you have? None of us knew."

"We could have done more tests, been more sure."

Now Rhiannon did shrug. "There are always more tests that can be done. There will always be things that get missed. That can't stop us from continuing to try to make things better. We were trying to make things better." Rhiannon's voice got very small, very quiet, as she added, "And we did. We made some things better."

Keida's face contorted into a complicated, scornful expression. "Not for the Hoilyn." She chewed on her lip, thinking, replaying her options that she'd already played over and over again in her mind, always coming to the same conclusion. Even so, she tried saying them out loud this time, out loud to someone who might be able to help her see a way out of the dead ended maze she'd found herself in. "I could move down to Da Vinci with the Hoilyn and keep studying how to fix this, but..."

"Your grants wouldn't carry over," Rhiannon provided. She knew how this game played out. "There would be no resources. No resources for studying a fairly small population of non-human aliens."

"Right." Keida frowned, frustrated. "I have all this money, and all this freedom... but only to a certain level."

"And then the leash of funding snaps tight," Rhiannon said. She didn't sound nearly bitter enough about such a bitter truth. Because she wasn't bitter. She was content to work on new projects and leave the Hoilyn trapped on a single world, trapped by them, unable to set foot—well, hoof—on a single spaceship, atmo-dome, or space station within the Human Expansion. They weren't human, they hadn't proliferated throughout the western spiral arm of the galaxy... they weren't a priority.

Keida's patience snapped. Something broke inside her, looking at Rhiannon and realizing the limits of her caring. It was the kind of break that once it happens, it never changes back. The wound might heal over, but the process of healing changes it irrevocably, scar tissue replacing what was there originally. Something inside Keida would never be the same.

"Doesn't it bother you that we live in a galaxy filled with all kinds of different aliens, but almost everyone here is human?" There was one insectile alien among the latest batch of new physicists. Though, from what Keida had heard, even she had been raised among humans on a human space station. Among all the other non-human scientists she could think of, none of them had stayed more than a year or two before leaving. And why was that? And why wasn't anyone here worried about it?

Rhiannon shrugged again. Her hair had fallen so far forward, Keida couldn't see the expression on her face. At all. But it didn't really matter what expression was there—guilt, frustration, sadness, irritation, or even simple indifference. They all added up to the same thing.

Rhiannon wasn't bothered enough by the effect their algae packs had on the Hoilyn to want to do anything about it. She didn't plan to study the harm they'd done together and try to reverse it. Maybe Keida could beg Rhiannon to work with her on the project, and maybe they would work together, fitfully, between other projects, squeezing it in, for a little while. But if Rhiannon didn't care, she wouldn't make it a priority. The work would dwindle. Nothing would get done.

And when it came down to it, Keida didn't know enough of the chemistry to work on improving their old project—redoing it, undoing it, fixing the problems with it—without Rhiannon's help. Maybe she could pressure some other chemist at Wespirtech to work with her, but if Rhiannon found the idea of the project uninspiring—and it had, at least, originally been her project, originally interested her—then why would any other chemist here be likely to find it interesting?

And they were all—all of them—only interested in working on what struck their fancy. They followed one idea to the next, not caring where those ideas led, or what meadows the paths they followed tore up along the way, as long as they kept leading somewhere interesting. They let science become them, all of them, leaving not enough behind to simply be a person.

Keida loved science, but she was more than science. More than a scientist. And she thought, maybe she'd outgrown her time at Wespirtech. It was a painful thought. She'd loved so much of her time there, but she wasn't interested in pursuing ideas in a vacuum, ignoring the effect they had on the world. The galaxy. She wanted to help people. To make a difference.

And that wasn't what Wespirtech was about. Pursuing science can be admirable, but for Keida, it was no longer enough.

Keida and Rhiannon talked about other subjects for a while, but it was the half-hearted conversation of friends who have drifted apart, who assure each other that they'll be closer going forward, and who don't follow through on those assurances.

Keida's mind was already elsewhere, thinking about an article she'd read about research biologists being needed in the asteroid belt of another star-system, thinking forward, and imagining the good that she might be able to do... somewhere else.

Wespirtech would be fine without her.

2

———

SLUG TIME

"Hey, Deenah, want to come down to the grav-lab with me? I hear the physics department is putting on a wild party tonight. Free-fall twister, skate around the edge of the black hole... That sort of thing."

Deenah put down the annulator she was using to fine-tune the wires in her hackishly made brain-wave generator. Wespirtech was legendary for its parties, and the physics department hadn't thrown one since Deenah arrived. She was sorely tempted to put her work aside and accompany Rayston...

"I can't," she said. "I have a project review tomorrow. If I get this working... get some visible progress..." she trailed off. "I'm afraid if I don't, they'll take my grant money away."

Rayston looked over the pair of brain-scanners, connected together by trailing wires. They looked like something you'd see in a hair salon: blue Naugahyde chairs with hollow metal boxes attached at the top, where the head goes. Except for the monitor screens in front. Chairs in a hair salon probably wouldn't have those.

"You want help with that?" Rayston asked, finishing his perusal.

Deenah was surprised. Rayston was a chemist; she didn't think he knew anything about brains. "With projecting a complex brain pattern from one creature into the brain of another?" she asked him. "In an interpretable form?"

"No, no, not with the neuro-stuff." He shuddered.

Deenah raised her eyebrows and gestured for Rayston to continue, but he was caught up in his head, imagining all the neuroscience he didn't know. "So..." Deenah prompted, "What kind of help did you mean?"

"Oh, spin," he said, as if that explained it all. Deenah rolled her eyes in impatience, and this time he caught on. "You know, spinning your project, so the grant analyst is blown away by how profitable it'll be and wants to give you lots of money to keep working on it."

"Spin?" Deenah said, incredulous.

"Yeah, spin. How do you think I get them to keep letting me work on cold fusion?"

That one *was* a mystery. Deenah tilted her head acknowledging his point. Yet, she didn't think spin alone could keep the government pouring money down the bottomless hole of cold fusion. No, Rayston had a knack for inventing useful objects along the way: endo- and exothermic candies, heat-wave trees, *marketable* science.

"No thanks," Deenah said. "I'm close. I can feel it. And, if I can just get this working—I'll be one step closer to making the translator work, and it doesn't take much spin to convince the government to fund work on a Universal Translator."

Rayston shrugged. "Suit yourself, but I'll be down at the grav-lab playing swoop-ball, if you change your mind." He pulled the door to the lab open and stepped through. It had almost shut behind him when he poked his head back in. "Oh, and feel free to wake me up any time tonight—I know how important grants are."

Deenah listened as Rayston's footsteps receded down the

hall. She suppressed the urge to follow him, and instead returned to connecting the wires between the two diagnostic brain-scanners she'd jerry-rigged together. "They'll throw another party..." she muttered to herself. "I wonder what swoop-ball is like?"

She uploaded her new edits to the software—a few debugs and a new algorithm for simplifying the test-subject's brain pattern.

"*This* time..." she said, looking at the test-subject: one of the biology department's color-changing cats. "This time, I'll find out what it's like to be a cat." The cat crouched, staring at her, green eyes fixed but every other color in its body flickering and melting as its tabby stripes crawled from the base of its ears down to the tip of its tail. The biologists called their new breed of scrolling-striped tabbies *Marquise* cats.

"It's a good thing you're cooperative," Deenah said to the Marquise, cranking a can-opener around a fresh can of tuna. She set the tuna can on the pile of boxes she'd used as a pedestal for the cat to stand on inside the brain-scanner. The bio-department didn't have any brain-scanners designed for animals. The boxes only wobbled a little as the cat jumped in, grinning and licking its chops.

"Better yet," Deenah said. "I'll find out what it's like to be a cat *eating a can of tuna*. Hmm. Maybe next time I'll find a little catnip to throw in..." She rechecked the connections, and then leaned back in her own brain-scanner.

The hum of the scanners powering up...

The brightly colored diagram of the cat's brain flickering to life on the other scanner...

The warm sensation of Deenah's scanner projecting the cat's brain-pattern onto hers...

Her ears burned as if she was blushing, and her eyes blurred for a moment. When her vision cleared, Deenah's ears burnt with the heat of a real blush. Her algorithm had failed.

Her brain was rejecting the projected waves—they were still incomprehensible.

"Damn!" Deenah yelled, slamming her fist against the arm of the brain-scanner chair. The cat startled and, done with the tuna, scurried away. "Damn!" There was no one in the room to rant about it to except the cat, slinking around the door, pawing the crack underneath, asking to be let out. So, Deenah made a tight-lipped frown and fumed quietly to herself.

"Okay, back to square-one." She went over to the terrarium where she kept simpler test-subjects. She'd had her best success with slugs, so far. It was easier dealing with animals whose neural pathways were already completely mapped. In fact, technically, slugs didn't even have brains, but their neural pathways were complicated enough to suffice as a control in her experiments.

She took one of the slugs out of the terrarium and placed it in a wide-mouthed petri-dish. She tore some greenery up for the slug to eat and set the whole shebang up on the box-pedestal. If the program worked on the slug, at least her code wasn't bugged. Deenah leaned back in the stiff Naugahyde medical chair attached to the scanner. She flicked the switches for both scanners and...

The hum of powering up...

The less bright and colorful diagram of a slug brain...

AND THEN DEENAH was the slug. She was still Deenah, and she still wished she were at the gravity party instead of working. But her arms were gone; her legs; her clothes; her vision was dim—a mere sense of the quality of light; and, the smell of ozone in the air and the plastic of the petri dish were like mountains before the eyes of a human. The program wasn't buggy. It just wasn't any good as a translator.

AFTER FIVE MINUTES, the scanners powered down. Deenah had put them on a timer, since she couldn't trust herself to remember to turn them off while being a slug, let alone find her fingers for operating the switch.

She started to push herself off of the sweaty, sticky Naugahyde, but hesitated. She knew she should get back to coding. She had a few ideas for new algorithms—ways to filter out the noise in a cat's brain, focusing on the frontal lobe and weeding out wave patterns related to the cat's own senses. The more she thought about it, the more overwhelmed Deenah felt. Perhaps another five minutes in the slug's brain would inspire a simpler solution...

MMM... *the simplicity of slugginess.*

AFTER THE FIVE MINUTES, Deenah had five fewer minutes until her project review and was no closer to inventing a working Universal Translator. But five minutes isn't much, and if the next five minutes gave her that Holy Grail—an inspired solution—it could save her hours of hard work.

LEAN BACK, *turn on, repeat.*

AN HOUR LATER, Deenah made it out of the Naugahyde chair and over to her computer where she tried to code for a while. She threw together a hack version of a new algorithm and tried it out on the slug, but her code was bugged and the program didn't work at all. Two hours of debugging fixed the code, but the new algorithm didn't work any better than the old one when she lured back the cat.

This time, Deenah heard whooping in the halls as she removed the slug from its terrarium. Rayston pushed his head through a crack in the door. She could hear Ivan, Anna, and Keida jostling and joking behind him. *Their* grants were all safe. They were all thoroughly funded. "Still working?" Rayston asked.

Deenah's pride was hurt too badly—having to work while the others played—to grace Rayston with a proper answer. She nodded curtly and kept her eyes on the slug. Its yellow back and black spots formed an almost obloid shape as the slug scrunched itself up, staying away from the edges of the petri dish. She centered the petri dish on the boxes, fussing with its position until she heard the door shut behind her. She could hear Rayston and the others, laughing as they descended down the hall.

She slammed her hands, open palmed, against the seat of her Naugahyde chair. The entire device wobbled, and she bit her lip realizing what a disaster it would be to knock the brain-scanner to the floor. These scanners were expensive, and *technically* they were both on loan from one of Keida's projects. Keida could afford brain-scanners.

In order to keep herself from asking the question, "Is Keida more successful than me because she's lucky, works harder, or because she's simply smarter?", Deenah punched a new number into the timer and turned the scanner on.

Muscles rippled along the sides of her stomach-foot. Her eyes twiddled at the ends of their stalks; her nose, like her eyes now, twiddled too. Her tongue, a spiky radula, flickered in and out of her mouth, sawing satisfyingly at the hearty-smelling greens.

She ate one leaf.

Then another.

And another.

When the machines powered down and Deenah remembered herself, she cursed herself inwardly for her caprice. Three hours ago, there might have been time to code, debug, and try out one more algorithm. Now, with only four hours left until her eight o'clock review—she checked her watch three times before she believed it—she only had time to sleep.

"Hey," came Rayston's voice from around the door. "How's it going?" He came in and held out a bag of his endothermic candies to her.

"Are those the cold ones or the hot ones?" Deenah asked, still trying to shake her three hours of slughood out of her brain.

Rayston looked down at the bag. "Endo," he said.

Deenah came over and took a handful. "I like these. They make me think of mochi ice cream." She bit in, and the pressure of her teeth broke the hard candy shell, launching the endothermic chain reaction that chilled the gooey center. "Strawberry."

"Mmm," Rayston agreed, chewing. "Have you invented a Universal Translator yet?"

"No." She took another handful of candies. "I spent the last three hours being a slug. Why are you up?"

"We were talking about lava flows in zero gee," Rayston said, still munching the endos, "and Keida went to see if she could find any geologists who knew how to actually model it. Then, it looked like Anna and Ivan might like to be left alone. So, I came to check on you. Is that the slug?" He gestured toward the brain-scanners with his bag of candy.

Deenah nodded, her mouth filled with cool strawberry cream.

"Can I try it?"

Deenah shrugged, and Rayston handed her his bag of candies so he could crawl into the chair and settle his head on the Naugahyde headrest, inside the gleaming metal and plastic contraption that picked up his brainwaves and projected new ones on top of them. Deenah checked the slug, reset the timer for five minutes, and then flicked the scanners on.

She watched Rayston's eyes glaze and his face grow lax. She pulled a desk chair over so she could keep an eye on him while the timer counted down. The monitor showed his brain waves in red and pink lines; the simulated slug brain waves were superimposed in blue. The blue lines were a mere tangle of yarn in front of the red and pink tapestry. The lines wobbled, tangled, stretched, and warped. Deenah began to drift to sleep watching them; she began to see shapes in the lines, and she dreamed that the lines pulled together and spelled out words. That was the key! She didn't need to project one person's brain waves onto another, merely find a way to translate those wavy lines directly into words on the screen...

THE TIMER CLICKED, and the scanners powered down. Rayston roused, blinked, shook his head. He didn't notice Deenah's drooping chin and closed eyes.

"Wow," he said. "That's relaxing."

Deenah woke with a start. "What?"

"Being a slug. It's *relaxing*." Rayston swung out of the chair and went over to scritch the Marquise cat still slinking in the corner. "You've got itchy ears," he said. Then, looking back at Deenah: "So, what is it about the project review that worries you?"

"Are you kidding?"

His blank look told her that he wasn't. Deenah took a deep breath and explained her fears. The words came out in one rush once she began. She'd never had a project review before; her project was too ambitious, and she had no proof she could ever accomplish it; all the other scientists around were constantly proving great things or inventing practical objects, and none of them even seemed to work as hard as she did.

"I should have finished testing at least five more algorithms by now... And, no matter what I do, it seems to be easier to translate sensory perceptions than actual *thoughts*." The frustration drained from Deenah as she spoke. She felt such relief in confiding it. But she was still tired. And it was still too late to have a working projection of a cat brain for tomorrow.

She caught the green eye of the Marquise cat, sitting by her computer and licking its paw. It remained as unknowable as cats have ever been.

Rayston followed her glance. "So, you can't do cats yet. So what? What animals can you do?" He went over to the terrarium and started poking around. "Bugs?" he asked. "It'd be great to have all those legs. *And wings.*" He grinned.

"Actually, it's really confusing," Deenah said. "I use the slug because there's less sensory information to process, so I can tell if I'm getting closer to translating the slug's thoughts."

"If a slug *has* thoughts," Rayston added, chortling. "*That* might be your problem." He plucked a centipede out of the terrarium. "Can I try being this guy?"

"Now?" Deenah asked with exasperation.

Rayston straightened up. "You're right. It's late." He put the centipede back. "The slug was good enough for tonight. But, you're gonna *have* to let me back in that chair some time." He caught her eye and leveled his gaze.

Deenah gave him a quizzical look. "I get it," she said. "You think I should spin this—" she gestured at the brain-scanners, terrarium, the whole room, her whole project, "as some kind of saleable product. *Buy the new Brain Box: Be a Slug and Know the Ultimate in Relaxation.*"

Rayston pointed at her and grinned. "Now you're getting it."

"But... These scanners are so expensive. Who would buy one just to find out what it's like to be a slug?"

Rayston looked at her levelly again, and Deenah felt pushed to find a way around the obstacle.

"Of course..." she said, thinking as she went, "you wouldn't need the whole scanner. I could simplify the projector... And pre-record the slug brainwaves. And maybe the brainwaves of a few other invertebrates that my algorithms can handle. I guess that wouldn't be so expensive." Deenah chewed on her lip, thinking it over. "I could get something like that working in a few weeks." She looked back up at Rayston. "But, would they really go for that? I mean, my grant is supposed to be funding a Universal Translator. Not some kid's toy."

"Of course," Rayston agreed. "And you're still working on that. You just happened to find this great spin-off technology along the way."

Rayston tossed her another endo-candy, and Deenah smiled.

"Now, get some sleep," Rayston said. "The government likes to think we scientists keep diurnal sleep schedules like the rest of the world. We don't want you so bleary eyed that you give us away."

"Thanks," Deenah said, and Rayston wished her good luck as he left her to tidying up the room.

She powered down the brain-scanners and her computer, thinking about everything Rayston had said. Maybe she wasn't so different from the other scientists. Just younger. He'd made her feel a part of the club.

Once the slug, her key to wowing the grant analyst, was safely returned to the terrarium, Deenah scooped up the Marquise on her way out. Surprised by the unexpected swooping, Marquise's claws dug in and tail fluffed out.

"You're too tense, kitty," Deenah chided as she hit the lights. "Maybe you should try being a slug too."

3

EINRAY AND THE BIOLOGIST

The elasti-tron was covered with dried and wilting plants again. Einray grumbled as he started peeling the putrid produce off of the glass sample plate. He hated the squishiness of biology.

"What are you guys doing in here?" Einray asked.

Brent Schweitzer and the other biologists looked amongst each other, waiting to see who would answer him. Finally, Brent gave in and became their representative. "The botany and gengineering labs are still shut down from the accident with Deenah's hallucinogenic moss."

One of the younger scientists glared at Brent. She must have been Deenah. "It wasn't an accident," she said. "It was *supposed* to transmit neuro-waves that would interfere with human brains." She dusted her hands off, but they stayed dirty from the potting soil she'd been shaking out of a flower's root system. "I just didn't think it would work," she said. "That's all."

Einray shuddered at the powdering of potting soil ringing around Deenah on the floor.

"Anyway..." Brent continued explaining, "it's really hard to decommission a plant that gives off *groovy* vibes to anyone who gets near it. For now, they've set up a field around the lab to cancel out the neuro-waves. But, until the moss dies off on its own, or someone can rig up a more refined way to cancel out the neuro-waves..."

"You'll be working here," Einray concluded, dismally. Biologists had no place in a physics lab. At least, not *his* physics lab.

But there was no way to avoid it. He was bumping shoulders with plant-laden practitioners of the squishy-sciences all day. And the next day. By the third day, he thought he'd give the day a skip. Instead, Einray came into the lab that *night*. He was deeply embroiled in measuring the vibrational density of elasti-tron generated chronoplasm, when the door to the lab swung open.

"Oh no," Einray groaned, "not at night too."

"I'll assume that was meant to be inaudible"; the answer came from Schweitzer. He made his way across the lab to the corner that the biologists had staked out for storing their flora. It was a veritable mini-jungle, barely hemmed in by the smooth, inorganic lines of the elasti-tron and its kin. "I'm just checking on the growth of my tree. I'll be out of your hair in a minute."

Against his better judgment, perhaps because he was tired, Einray found himself saying, "You have to come in at night to do that? I'd think a *tree* would grow slowly enough to wait until morning."

After a bit of rustling around in the corner, Schweitzer emerged, disappointment on his face. "It would seem, you're right."

"I suppose you're trying to make a super fast growing tree," Einray said, realizing that he was coming dangerously close to expressing interest. He balanced it out by adding, "How mind-numbingly practical."

"I suppose it might be," Schweitzer muttered, paying more attention to the chrono-logger he was fiddling with than to

Einray. "But, then, so is this, and I believe you're the one who invented it?" He shot Einray a glance, around the side of the sleek metal machine.

"Yes," Einray answered, "But I needed a way to change sub-atomic particle velocities without observing them for my experiments. Other people came up with all the practical uses later."

"Ah, I see," Brent said. "You kept your hands clean." He stood up, flicking the switch that turned the chrono-logger off.

"What are you doing using the chrono-logger anyway?" This time Einray couldn't help feeling intrigued, and conveyed the feeling through his voice.

"I figured," Brent said, "as long as I'm stuck in the physics lab, I might as well see if there's a way to use all this physics stuff," he gestured around at all the giant, metal boxes—elasti-tron, chrono-logger, and their ilk—, "in my work."

"And?" Einray prompted. Anything involving his giant physics machines interested him

"So far, no luck."

Einray started to make a derisive comment, but he found it stuck in his throat. So, instead he asked, "Are you sure you were using it right?" Coming over to the far side of the lab, he flicked the chrono-logger back on and checked all its settings.

"What's wrong?" Schweitzer asked after watching Einray frown at it for a minute.

"What?" Einray said. "Oh... Nothing. These settings are fine." He didn't bother mentioning how surprised this made him. "What are you using it on?"

"Here, I'll show you," Schweitzer said, sliding a glass sample plate under an adjacent microscope. Six hours later, the dawn lights flickered on around the edges of the ceiling.

The dawn lights didn't make it any brighter per se, but they changed the *quality* of the lab's lighting. It was a clever idea from the administration: they hoped to enforce (or at least encourage) a semblance of a diurnal schedule on Wespirtech and its scientists by simulating the difference between natural daytime and unnatural nighttime light. With all the Wespirtech scientists working in underground labs on an un-atmosphered moon, even the "natural" daytime light was artificial.

Schweitzer and Einray were unfazed by the change in lighting. They had lined up a dozen petri dishes on the lab table. Each hosted an Altarian Ash seed, and the two scientists were carefully grafting their doctored zygotes into the seeds. It had been a long and tedious process.

Sure, the first part was fun and easy: run zygote after zygote through the chrono-logger at every setting imaginable. Einray had gone completely crazy making up weird combinations of quark vibrations to impress Schweitzer. Of course, the altered zygotes themselves were completely useless until they'd been treated with pheno-transcriptase to create DNA-containing cells that would be capable of replicating themselves and then spliced into viable Altarian Ash seeds.

But, by that point, Einray was hooked. So, there he found himself, hours later, poking at a tiny, fleshy green thing, trying to make his clumsy fingers work the tweezers properly. "Dammit!" he cried as his fingers slipped for the dozenth time.

"Hey, Jon, you look exhausted," Schweitzer said. "I can finish up here, if you'd like to get some breakfast. Or maybe... go to bed."

"Breakfast?" Einray said with distate. "After staying up all night?"

"That's the best part of staying up all night," Schweitzer said. "Eating breakfast before you go to bed."

"Thanks but no thanks," Einray answered. He skipped filling his stomach with sugary pancakes and greasy eggs. Einray went straight to bed.

The next morning—well, afternoon—Einray hit the lab and his first question, to the first person he saw, was: "Where's Schweitzer?"

Deenah answered, "You just missed him."

It took a moment for Einray to realize, with a sinking feeling, what Deenah meant. Schweitzer had just now gone to bed. And he wouldn't be up, probably, for another eight hours.

"But... I want to know how the chrono-logged Ash are doing."

Deenah shrugged, unhelpfully, and Einray scowled at her. He'd have to dig through the biologists' little corner jungle and find his physics-ized plants himself. He hoped Schweitzer had labeled them properly.

Einray needn't have worried. An entire row of seed-pots lined the far wall, each bearing a carefully printed label reading "Altarian Ash, 67-11, 9am" followed by the specifications of the chrono-logger settings for that particular seed.

Most of the pots sported a tiny, green sproutling in the middle of the dark, moist potting soil. Those didn't interest Einray. One pot did. The tree in that one was the absolute perfect size for the pot. Approximately a foot tall, bushing out at the sides like a little tree should. "It's a good thing Brent didn't plant you in anything smaller," he said, examining the plant. (Without touching it. Instead, he poked it with his chemi-pen.)

Einray wondered if he should re-pot the tree himself, but he decided not. Clearly, that tree had already served its purpose. Now Einray knew what settings to focus on with the chrono-logger. The next seed would grow even faster.

The next several days, Einray and Schweitzer worked long hours on the chrono-logged Ash, communicating almost entirely by notes. They shared a few bleary, mismatched meals —Einray eating breakfast, while Schweitzer finished dinner, or vice versa—but mostly they worked alone.

By the end of the week, they were planting the seeds in the atrium rather than pots. It wasn't the ideal environment. Since the entire Wespirtech complex was built under an atmospheric bubble on the Da Vinci moon, the soil in the atrium only went so deep. Under that, it was hard moon rock. Still, the two men marveled at their work. Before they'd begun, the atrium was a grassy courtyard. Its only plants were experiments, mostly small bushes and flowers like Deenah's foxcups and butter-gloves. Now, it was a veritable indoor forest. The dome and starry sky above were barely visible through thick, green Ash leaves.

The two men shared a rare moment together, staring up at the trees. Einray's hands were dirty, but he didn't mind. It gave him a funny feeling, looking at all these living things... knowing that he'd made them. Clean, pure, abstract, infinitesimal physics had grown under his guiding hands into this vibrant mass of green.

"That was... fun," he said. "I guess we're done now."

"I'm going to my sister's wedding..." Schweitzer said.

"Archaic tradition," Einray, the confirmed bachelor, said in response to Schweitzer's bizarre non sequitur.

"It's down on Da Vinci," Schweitzer continued without missing a beat. "I could take some seeds and see how they do down there. That's the next step of our experiment. Maybe show it to some corporate sponsors. See if we can get a grant to continue our research."

Einray balked. "I don't know that I want my name on a biology grant." What he really meant was that the idea of dealing with corporate sponsors of any type made him queasy.

Schweitzer rolled his eyes. "Grants are always good. Besides, it'll make an excellent wedding present. I'll plant the seed right before the ceremony... And, when we come out," he swooshed his hands toward the sky, "there'll be a beautiful tree standing in its place."

Einray wasn't there, but he could tell something had gone wrong—horribly wrong—all the way from orbit.

"What the hell?" Deenah said. She'd been gazing out the window of the cafeteria, staring at the blue and green globe of Da Vinci that was rising over Wespirtech as she ate.

Einray was sitting at the far end of the same long table. He'd been spending more time around the biologists lately. He wasn't a man of many friends, and his collegial collaboration with Schweitzer had made him feel more beneficent toward the entire biology profession. So, when Deenah exclaimed, he actually looked up and glanced out the window.

Along the shadowed curve of night on Da Vinci, the lights were going out. The cities were twinkling into darkness, and, though Einray couldn't be sure his eyes weren't playing tricks on him, he thought the rest of the central continent, that was still in daylight, was subtly shifting to a different shade of green.

"Einray! Jonathan Einray! Report to a com-station at once!" the intercom blared, and Einray jumped up without even putting his utensils down. The message repeated, following Einray down the halls of Wespirtech, until he reached his room and punched on the com, fork and knife still in hand.

It was Schweitzer on the com-screen. It looked like he was using a wrist-com, and there were trees, *visibly growing*, behind him.

Einray unconsciously mimicked Deenah: "What the hell?!" he said.

"So, I planted a seed..." Schweitzer answered, his voice coming through fuzzy from the wrist-mic.

"And?"

"Um... This?" Schweitzer threw his arm around, giving Einray a wobbly but more complete view of Schweitzer's surroundings.

Schweitzer seemed to be standing in front of a church—

probably the site of his sister's wedding. The steps from the sidewalk, the street corner, and, even the church itself, were all being overgrown. Trees sprouted around Schweitzer, piercing right through the pavement—*right through the buildings*. People ran about in confusion and hysteria. Schweitzer even jumped to the side, dodging a new seedling that sprouted under his very feet.

"Your chrono-logger did a lot more to those seeds than we realized. It must have. I'd laugh... but this is a natural disaster beyond all proportions."

Einray stared, far from blankly, at the com-screen. Sub-sub-atomic particles juggled and rearranged themselves in his mind. "I know what's happening," he said.

"Great!" Schweitzer said. "'Cause, I'm at a complete loss."

"I don't know how to fix it."

There was a pause. The trees kept growing.

"*Stupid biologist,*" Einray muttered.

"I know, I should have tested it in a controlled environment." Schweitzer's voice bespoke the infinite, infinitely tested patience of someone who *needs* something.

"You shouldn't have tested it at all."

"If you can't fix it, maybe I can. Just *explain* it to me."

"Right..." Einray's eyes were focused on the air in front of the com-screen. He was still juggling particles and quantum states in the imaginary workspace in his head. "I'll try..." he said. Explaining quantum sub-physics to a biologist wouldn't be easy. "But I'm going to get a shuttle. And I'll tell you about it while I fly down."

"Is that a good idea—?" Schweitzer tried to ask, but he found himself talking to an empty wrist-screen. By the time Einray flickered back to place, a tiny image on Schweitzer's wrist-screen, he was already en route to Da Vinci, and he immediately launched into an in-depth, improvised lecture on the nature of piggybacked quantum states and how they effected chrono-logged sub-particles.

Schweitzer didn't get a chance to mention his concern—namely that one of them should be at Wespirtech with access to all their equipment there—until both men had their feet firmly on the quaking surface of Da Vinci. By then, his concern was completely forgotten, swept away by all-consuming scientific awe.

"You're saying..." said a tuxedo-clad Schweitzer to Einray as he emerged from the shuttle. (The rest of the wedding party had long since fled.) "You're saying that... *No*. That doesn't make sense."

"I assure you," Einray said, in the same matter of fact tone he always used, almost as if he wasn't ducking errant tree limbs while doing so, "This is the only explanation."

"But..." Schweitzer looked around at the trees, growing unthinkably around him. "If you're saying what I think you're saying, then these trees are travelling *backward in time* as they grow."

"Yes."

"And the seeds they're producing... *in the past*... are growing, *backward in time*, and producing more seeds and more *backward* growing trees."

"Exponentially."

"And, of course, they didn't do this on the moon, because it's fundamentally inhospitable. And our atrium hasn't been there very long," Schweitzer said.

"Only twenty-three years."

"Not enough history to travel through. That's..." Schweitzer paused a moment, swallowed the words, *really cool*, and instead said, "...*terrible*." Stepping aside as a seedling rapidly developed into the size of a healthy shrub at his feet, Schweitzer added, "We need a way to stop them."

"Obviously."

"In the past."

"Unless we want to leave the city destroyed. Like it is right now," Einray said, looking around at what was really more of a forest than a city. And an eerily quiet one. Most of the people had already fled, though he could hear occasional sirens in the distance.

The buildings that were still visible between the trees had taken on the aspect of ancient ruins, crumbling from the stab wounds inflicted by trees that had grown straight through their hearts. Piercing from underneath, the trees shot straight through the buildings' roofs and their branches crowded out through broken windows. "We need to work fast."

"We need equipment," Schweitzer said.

"And an idea," Einray countered.

"And *equipment.*"

"Equipment's no problem. My aunt has a laboratory on the other side of Confucius Canyon—that'll be somewhat shielded from the spread of the trees. She's an amateur *botanist.*" Einray said the word dismissively. "But she dabbles with real sciences on the side. I'll lead the way."

They left the intra-orbital shuttle parked by the church. It was inefficient for close-range, planetary travel. Fortunately, along with an array of differently sized spacesuits, the shuttle's supply closet was equipped with several collapsible supersonic hovercycles.

Einray and Schweitzer rode down city streets being shredded by roots that buckled pavement. The trees thinned, however, as they fled ground zero. The fleeing hordes, though, had gathered at the edge of town. Where paved streets turned to dirt roads, and city come forest turned into tree-sprinkled farmland.

Einray felt nervous riding through the crowds. But no one knew that the two men on hovercycles were behind this all... Fortunately. He feared to think what might happen if they knew. Images flitted through his mind of being dragged from his cycle and thrown to the ground, restrained, beaten, screamed at...

But, no one paid them heed, and the two men were soon cycling at full speed past the fields. As they rounded the canyon, the invading trees were barely a noticeable presence. Yet, a single glance over his shoulder told Einray that these golden, agrarian fields were on borrowed time.

Leaping off his hovercycle almost before the engine powered down, Einray dropped the conveyance on his aunt's lawn. Schweitzer followed suit and pursued Einray in his dead run around the red painted ranch house. The greenhouse out back was unlocked, and Einray went right in.

"I guess, Auntie Einray is quite the dabbler," Schweitzer said in awe as he entered.

Einray had already powered up a surprising array of equipment, and even more machines sat dormant on tables farther back, mixed right in with the hothouse plants.

"Aunt *Janice*, actually," a feminine voice said from behind. When Schweitzer turned to see her, the owner of the voice was a small woman with silver hair and thick, antique-style glasses. They could have been actual antiques, except for the slight shimmer that gave away the data stream hidden inside them. Auntie Einray might be old, but she was armed to the teeth— or, more precisely, the eyes—with hi-tech technology.

She shook Schweitzer's hand, but she swatted Einray on the back of the head. "This is what it takes? A natural disaster beyond all proportion, and finally you come for a visit."

Einray shot his aunt an irritated glance and directed himself at Schweitzer, "We could trigger a chain reaction in a lump of chrono-unstable trilonium. That would release a massive amount of radiation, slightly displaced in time to both the past and future."

Aunt Janice swatted her nephew on the back of his head again.

"What?" he said. "That would kill the trees!"

"That would kill every living thing on the planet," she said. "*Slightly displaced in time*, so we'd die in both the past and future."

"Fine. I could entrap the radiation in a fluctuating field that..." he trailed off. "No... that wouldn't work..." And Einray was lost again to the flickering readouts on all the machinery around him.

"I think I'm out of my depth here," Schweitzer said, looking at the machines Einray had powered up. "But," he said, pointing further into the greenhouse, "That looks more to my liking. Do you mind?"

Aunt Janice walked right over and started powering up the section of her laboratory devoted to biology. "Though, I'm surprised any friend of my nephew's would be interested in *these*."

"Indeed," Schweitzer acknowledged. He pulled some crumpled leaves and a chip of bark from his pocket and immediately started separating them into different samples for analysis. Test tubes, petri dishes, enzyme dispensers, and everything else he needed was readily available. Aunt Janice kept an excellent workspace.

"These samples are from the trees?" she asked. "The trees taking over the city?"

Schweitzer caught her up while running his samples. Collecting data was routine, and he could have done it in his sleep. Once he had the data, however... "I have no idea what to do with this."

Einray spoke up: "We need to collapse the time wave function that allows the trees to... um..." he couldn't really avoid saying it, "*time travel.*"

"No kidding," Aunt Janice said. "Boy, you sure should have stayed away from biology. I guess, it was some kind of second sight that made you hate it so."

Einray rolled his eyes.

Schweitzer shrugged. "If I had any idea how to do that, I'd be helping you here."

"I could do it... An EM pulse, filtered to oscillate in the time dimension... But, I can't be sure that wouldn't scramble everyone's brains in the process."

"Scramble?" Schweitzer said.

"You know, if you wanted to work with trees," Aunt Janice said, "I don't know why you couldn't have started on something simple. Like helping me save Stevie's sycamore from those dreadful root-moths."

Einray ignored his aunt's heckling. "An EM pulse polarized like that... Of the necessary magnitude...."

"Yeah, yeah. I get the idea," Schweitzer said. "No more trees, but a planet full of zombies."

"Actually, the trees would be fine. They'd just stop time-travelling. So the city would stay a forest. But the rest of the planet would be saved!"

"Uh huh." Aunt Janice looked unimpressed.

Schweitzer looked like he'd stopped listening. "What was that you said about root-moths?"

"Deadly things," Aunt Janice said. "Beautiful like butterflies, but they lay their eggs in the roots of sycamore trees. My husband Stevie had a sycamore he loved..." Aunt Janice turned away a little, even though her thick glasses mostly hid her eyes. "Anyway, the root-moths got to it. The poor thing just withered away and died. He used to sit under that tree for hours..." There was a catch in her voice, "Reading... out under his tree..."

The catch in her voice caught her nephew's attention, but he didn't know what to say. So, in an uncharacteristic show of thoughtfulness, the awkward, middle-aged scientist took his elderly aunt's hand and put his other hand heavily on her shoulder.

"That's terrific..." Schweitzer muttered.

"Excuse me?" Einray said.

"Janice, do you have any of those moths? Or moth eggs?"

Aunt Janice took her hand away to dab at her eyes.

"Don't be ridiculous," Einray said.

"Actually..." Aunt Janice said, "I saved some. For my moth collection."

Einray gaped at her.

"I *said* they were beautiful."

"Are any of them—"

Aunt Janice cut Schweitzer off, "*Alive*, yes. I see where you're going." She shuffled deeper into the greenhouse to a worktable overflowing with the draping greenery of her exotic, gengineered plants. She pulled out a drawer and removed a small, flat box. "I have dead ones, pinned. But, you'll want these."

Schweitzer took the box from her and flipped open the clear plastic lid. There were pinhead sized, oblong, yellow eggs inside. A bunch of them.

"I was trying to gengineer the moths out of killing trees."

Schweitzer looked up, startled.

"Don't worry," Aunt Janice said. "I didn't succeed."

The chrono-logger was already powered up, and Einray remembered the final settings they'd used on the Altarian Ash seeds exactly. Nonetheless, he made a big show of fiddling with the chrono-logger's knobs and dials to avoid being conscripted into helping with the icky, squishy moth eggs. Aunt Janice would make a better assistant for Schweitzer anyway. Her fingers were smaller.

When Einray could see that his companions were deeply involved, he slipped outside.

Already, the forest was coming.

If it were a person, it would be knocking on Aunt Janice's back door. Short sprigs of treelings littered her lawn. The farther away, the taller they were. Approximately two fields away, the Ashes towered to the sky, as if they were reaching toward Wespirtech. Einray pictured the monstrous trees reaching all the way to his safe little home on the moon, and pulling it down. His pristine life in the metal halls, buried in the dead crater of a sterile moon—dragged into a mire of living, green, carbon-dioxide breathing hell.

Einray stood transfixed, mesmerized.

"We've got them!" Schweitzer shouted. "I hope they work..."

The biologist and the amateur dabbler came running past Einray.

"Do to those trees what you did to Stevie's sycamore!"

"And more!"

Einray stumbled as a stubborn seedling sprouted under his foot. Another tree, almost head high, shoved him with its branches. Meanwhile, Aunt Janice and Schweitzer were scrabbling frantically at the ground, burying their precious moth eggs as deep in the roots as they quickly could.

"How long..." Aunt Janice began to ask, but her question needed no voice. Before she began to spoke, the moth eggs, responding to cues from the moisture and minerals in the soil awoke. Tiny caterpillar-like bugs hatched, gnawed on the roots, grew big, burrowed out of the ground—all backwards in time. Their chrysalises hid in the bark at the base of their victim trees. They grew wings, flew away, laid more eggs...

The whole cycle spiraled backward and outward in time. The trees themselves had traveled already back to the time the continents broke apart. Giant slug-like aliens had crawled across the surface of Da Vinci then. They'd never known trees. Not until Schweitzer and Einray sent them the Altarian Ash.

Then, suddenly, they knew butterflies.

From end to end of their timeline, the Altarian Ash were

eaten away. Their strong trunks grew mottled. Their leaves turned withered and red. More and more, brilliant golden wings unfolded from the hidden crevices in their trunks and took to flight.

To Aunt Janice's eyes, an entire forest burst into golden, beating flame. The flapping of the moths wings was a wind, and, then, they were gone.

With all the trees dead, from the beginning of time, there was nowhere for their eggs to have grown... They vanished in a beautiful paradox.

"Wow," the word was mere breath, and before it was spent, the memory that caused it was gone. "That..." Aunt Janice groped for an understanding of why her nephew had brought a biologist friend of his to visit her and show off her laboratory. Exasperated to find none, she offered the men some tea and bid her nephew a fond farewell when he turned her offer down.

Schweitzer and Einray parted ways in town. Schweitzer still had a wedding reception to attend, and Einray felt an urgent need to escape him. Although his memories of recent circumstances were gone, the feelings inspired by them... lingered.

"Let's not... do anything with those seeds we made," Schweitzer said as Einray boarded the shuttle.

"No," he agreed. "Let's not." In fact, although he didn't say it, Einray firmly planned to destroy them. And all the records of their creation.

As the shuttle rose through the atmosphere and Einray felt the safety of his home and his own small room coming closer, the dread he'd felt on the planet began to recede. He was glad Schweitzer accepted now that the Altarian Ash adventure was over. That talk of grants and funding was all crazy talk.

But... It had been an adventure. Hadn't it? Maybe it wouldn't be so bad to work with a biologist again.

4

___

MY WORDS LIKE SILENT RAINDROPS

Nicole and Ivan were among the newest, promising young scientists at the Western Spiral Arm Planetary Institute of Technology. For the time being, they were working on a project together. He did the chemistry, and she did the physics. The partnership worked well. Almost too well.

This morning, while warming up the elasti-tron, Nicole cruised through the Wespirtech history files to pass the time. They *meant* to get an early start, but the old vid-files were too funny. By the time the elasti-tron made its *blink, blink, beep, beep, I'm ready* signal, Nicole and Ivan were deeply absorbed and didn't notice.

"Look at this folder," Nicole said to Ivan, who was watching over her shoulder. "These vids are absolutely ancient...all the way back from when people lived on Earth I..." They shook their heads appreciatively.

"Mindular telechips..." Ivan read. "I wonder what that is..."

Intrigued, Nicole opened the folder and played the first vid-file. After a series of credits and graphics, a middle-aged man with gray hair appeared on the screen and introduced himself as Alan Alda.

"It started out harmlessly enough," Alan Alda said. "Jason Middleton, a student at MIT and part of a group called the MIT cyborgs, designed the original implant as a receiver for an mp3 radio station he ran off of his wearable computer." The speaker's voice continued, but the video showed an image of a young man with a computer strapped on at his waist and a tiny monitor eye patch covering one eye. "The implant played music straight into Jason's brain. He called it a *Mindleton*, as a play on his own name, and convinced all of his cyborg buddies to get them too."

Here, the video showed an image of a bunch of cyborgs, fully outfitted in their wearable computers, walking around the MIT campus and banging their heads to the same inaudible music. Nicole and Ivan burst out laughing. Meanwhile, Alan Alda explained how a cell phone company recently purchased rights to Jason's patent and changed the product's name to the *Mindular Telechip*. After discussing telechip construction with Jason and future mindular possibilities with a representative of the cell phone company, Alan Alda ended the section with these words:

"Might these telechips be the next step in human evolution? In twenty years, will we all be, essentially, telepathic? Where *are* you taking us, Alexander Graham Bell?"

After that, the vid-file cut out, with a note that the rest of the program was available but contained no information on mindular telechips.

"Who's Alexander Grambell?" Ivan wondered, but Nicole paid him no heed and started up the next vid-file. It was labeled a *tv-ad*. There were several, actually, and Nicole ran all of them. The first featured a husband and wife at a stuffy cocktail party.

The wife, cornered by an annoying neighbor, sends a

message to her husband. He tilts his head, showing he can hear her plea for help; then he walks over and rescues her from the boor. The piece ends with the slogan: "Mindular Telechip: *Get Even Closer*." The rest of the *tv-ads* were pretty much the same.

"Cute," Ivan said when they were all over. "Looks like it was just a fad."

Nicole didn't respond. She was deep in thought.

"Nicole?" Ivan asked. "You okay?"

"You know what?" she said. "We should make some of those."

"You kidding?" Ivan asked.

"The concept is pretty simple..."

"Sure, I could probably hobble something together in a few days. I'm pretty good with electronics. But why?"

"Think of how much fun it would be! We could walk around secretly talking to each other. The admins wouldn't have a clue what's going on!"

"Admin has no clue what's going on anyway," Ivan said.

"Just do it?" Nicole pleaded.

"Sure," Ivan agreed. "If you say so."

Nicole flashed a brilliant grin. "Great, I have to go tell Cora."

CORA WAS IN HER ROOM, feeding the pet sea-bunny Nicole had given her. The sea-bunny was jumping about contentedly in its tank, splashing fitfully.

"Cora," Nicole said, out of breath leaning against the doorframe. "Would you like to be telepathic?"

"You're out of breath. Have you been running?" Cora asked.

"Ran all the way from the elasti-tron lab..." Nicole puffed. "Would you like to be telepathic?" she repeated.

"You were working with Ivan on the elasti-tron?" Cora asked.

"Sure, you know we're studying string dimensionality together."

Cora sighed. "My research hasn't been going anywhere lately. I haven't done anything of interest to the admins since they brought me here, and I've been here a lot longer than you. It must be easier with a partner."

"You haven't been here that long," Nicole said, feeling flustered. "You know, you could work with Ivan and me. There's plenty of physics in our project to support two physicists. The super dimensionality of strings is really challenging. There's a certain elasticity that..."

Cora broke in: "I'd feel too intimidated working with Ivan."

"Really?" Nicole said, genuinely surprised. "Ivan's so easygoing. Like a big teddy bear. I'm sure you'd get used to him. And I'd love to have your help."

Cora turned back to fiddling with the sea-bunny tank and said, "Don't worry, I'm sure if I keep working hard I'll come up with something."

Nicole wanted to help. If Cora would join her and Ivan on the elasti-tron project...Nicole would gladly share the credit, even for the work she'd already done. But forcing Cora didn't seem right. Perhaps it was best. The other scientists could be such sticklers for credit; they'd have probably thought it odd. "So, telepathy..." Nicole said, returning to the original topic. Maybe that would cheer Cora up.

BY THE TIME Ivan finished making the telechips, Nicole had convinced Cora to join them in their fun if not their research project. The three of them tried the telechips first, before telling any other scientists. Nicole had a plan.

Wespirtech's one dining hall served the scientists, admins, and other workers alike. Of course, the groups usually kept to themselves. Nonetheless, the admins liked to keep an eye on the scientists, and subscribed to the theory that their arrangement kept the scientists better socialized than if left entirely to themselves.

When Nicole, Cora, and Ivan arrived at the dining hall for lunch, each equipped with a new telechip, they fanned out. Cora and Ivan seated themselves at separate tables among scientists as far across the hall from the admins as they could. Nicole found a place much closer to the admins' table.

Once they'd been there awhile and made a good start on their lunches, Nicole got up and walked straight over to the admins' table, holding her hand as if it held a blaster.

"Prefect Osterio," she said to the admin who usually reviewed her work. "I've got something to show you. I know I should wait and make an appointment, but it's just so exciting..."

Pre. Osterio lowered her glasses a little, looking at Nicole's empty hand. Her expression conveyed the message, "Well, this should be a good one."

"See," Nicole continued, "I've managed to create an invisible, weightless blaster. Would you like to hold it?"

Pre. Osterio continued looking skeptical over the top of her glasses and didn't answer.

"Oh," Nicole added, "It's also completely silent. Here, watch." Nicole turned to the crowd of diners and pointed her "blaster" towards Ivan's back, supposedly at random. She thought the message, "Ivan, on three... one... two... three..." through her telechip.

Ivan was a good forty feet away, but he spasmed and fell out of his chair right as Nicole mimed pulling the trigger. There was quite an uproar at his table, and even something of an uproar among the admins.

Pre. Osterio stayed seated and skeptical, but the young man next to her, who'd been working at Wespirtech less time than Nicole had been researching there, jumped up, all excited.

"Sit down," Pre. Osterio commanded. "When you've been here a little longer, you'll see that the scientists have a penchant for pranks. Their research is generally the only thing they take seriously. If you really want to know how she did it, just wait a few weeks and ask. By then, I'm sure she'll be proud to explain it to you."

The new admin looked chagrined.

"You don't believe me?" Nicole asked, feigning surprise. "I can do it again..." Nicole repeated the same stunt, this time with Cora. The excitement among the scientists went up another notch, but Pre. Osterio still didn't look impressed.

"Okay, your loss," Nicole said. "I'll just have to sell them on the black market."

Pre. Osterio looked mildly amused by that, but she made no move to stop Nicole from leaving and returning to her lunch.

Nicole, however, could hardly keep herself from skipping with elation. She was dying to hear what all the scientists were saying at the other tables. She had to settle for listening to Cora's and Ivan's mindular reports.

"Everyone wants to know what just happened," Cora said, mindularly.

"Really? What are they saying? What are you saying?" Nicole mindulared back.

"I'm telling everyone to talk to Ivan privately if they're really interested. Just like we planned," Cora said.

"I'm gonna be so busy..." Ivan added, jumping in.

THE FIRST SCIENTIST TO seek Ivan out privately and ask about the stunt in the dining hall wasn't one of the younger scientists now, but, when he'd come to Wespirtech at the age of fifteen, he was the youngest they'd ever accepted. Having been at

Wespirtech, interacting almost exclusively with other scientists, for most of his life, Einray could be a little odd. Still, the plan Nicole, Cora, and Ivan had worked out was that they'd give telechip implants to anyone who really wanted them. It wasn't their intention to be exclusive.

After Einray, a few of the solar biologists, an eccentric lot, joined the growing group of telepaths. By the end of the week, the group of telepaths totaled nine in all: Nicole, Cora, Ivan, Einray, three solar biologists, a chemist friend of Ivan's, and another physicist named Anna Karlingoff.

At first, the telepaths thought their lives would go on as usual; that the telechips were just a novel oddity. However, Ivan set up the telechips so that a message sent through one telechip would be received by all the others. So, whenever one of the telepaths said anything mindularly, all the others heard it. The growing and ongoing presence of their mindular conversation drew the telepaths closer and closer together.

In fact, barely a week and a half after the original invisible blaster stunt, the nine telepaths were eating all their meals together. This is how it worked:

Whenever a meal was approaching, one or another of the telepaths would mindularly note feeling hungry. The other eight, once started thinking about it, would soon be hungry too. They'd debate it awhile, coordinating across the entire span of Wespirtech, and, eventually all nine telepaths would march into the dining hall within minutes of each other.

And, of course, the telepaths sat together. It was easier that way. Their mindular conversation would rage on all through lunch either way. When they sat together, normal conversation, among the non-telepaths, didn't interfere with their mindular conversation.

So, there the nine of them were: sitting around a table, eating silently, occasionally all breaking into spontaneous laughter together. The admins, the workers, and even the other scientists gave them very weird looks.

"IT'S FUN, ISN'T IT?" Nicole said to Cora, in normally voiced words.

The two of them were having a private, best friend type conversation in Cora's room. Nicole was lying on her stomach, on Cora's bed, kicking her feet in the air above her head. Cora was tending to the flopsy, splashy sea-bunny.

"I knew it'd be fun to get Ivan to make these chips…" Nicole continued, "but I really had no idea just how neat it would be. I mean, would we have ever really got to know the solar biologists? And Anna…I'm really getting to be friends with her."

Cora looked up from her aquatic ministrations. "Really? Anna?" Cora said. "She's kind of pretentious."

"She is more reserved…" Nicole agreed cautiously. "But, I think it might just be because she's older. She's been here several years longer than either of us."

"I suppose," Cora said, putting the lid on her sea-bunny's tank. "But that's not a very good reason. Maybe she's just nicer around you."

The skin between Nicole's eyebrows furrowed as she thought about Cora's words. Cora could seem really paranoid sometimes. First she was worried about Ivan; now about Anna. Nicole wished she could help Cora be less insecure.

Just then, Cora and Nicole heard one of the solar biologists say mindularly: "Telepaths! S'mores! We've got the makings in the solarity lab, and the flames look perfect for mallow-roastin'!"

"Want to go?" Nicole asked, jumping off the bed, and looking expectantly at Cora. For a moment, Cora looked tempted. Then, they heard Anna's mindular reply, saying she was on her way.

"No, that's okay," Cora said. "I've got reading to do."

"Come on," Nicole urged. "Maybe you'd get to know Anna a little better, and you wouldn't be so afraid of her."

Cora stiffened and turned away. Nicole felt bad about leaving. She knew Cora pretty well, though, and she suspected there wasn't anything she could do. Cora just needed to sulk sometimes.

"Save a marshmallow for me," Nicole mindulared, giving Cora a squeeze on the shoulder as she left.

THE NEXT MORNING, Nicole slept in. The s'more party had run late, and then Nicole stayed up even later talking to Anna. So, although she heard the other telepaths gathering for breakfast, she stayed in bed, dozing through the mindular breakfast conversation.

When Nicole finally got up, she went straight to the elasti-tron lab, hoping to see Ivan. They were close to a breakthrough, and she was hoping to report their findings to Pre. Osterio soon. Unfortunately, Ivan wasn't there. He hadn't been at the s'more party either. Nicole hadn't seen much of him at all lately.

"Ivan?" she mindulared irritably. "Has anyone seen Ivan? Ivan, where are you?"

Ivan didn't reply, but Einray mindulared: "I saw Ivan leaving Cora's room this morning."

Cora's room? Nicole thought. Come to think of it, Nicole realized that Cora and Ivan had been spending a lot of time together lately. Was that why Cora had been so intimidated by him? She *liked* him?

Einray continued, unprompted: "So, he's probably sleeping, 'cause it didn't look like he'd got much sleep when I saw him."

"Einray, you idiot!" Nicole mindulared. "Everyone can hear you." This interchange was followed by a titter of mindular laughter from the solar biologists, but none of the other telepaths said anything.

Nicole thought a bit more about Cora and Ivan together...she kind of liked the idea. Maybe Cora would be less insecure with a boyfriend. That would make her easier to take. "Sorry, Einray," Nicole mindulared. "I shouldn't have called you an idiot."

AFTER THAT DAY, Cora hung around the elasti-tron lab whenever Nicole and Ivan were working. She didn't help with the physics. She just hung off of Ivan's arm like a coat. At first it was sweet, then it was sickening.

"Come on guys," Nicole said, less than patiently. "Can we get some work done? I want to have this ready to show Pre. Osterio by the end of the week."

"Sorry," Ivan muttered, stepping back to the elasti-tron controls. Cora sat down in a rolley chair and began spinning, ostensibly reading the physics treatise in her lap. Her antics were clearly inordinately cute as far as Ivan was concerned. He was soon back at her side.

Nicole ignored them, glaring at her work. After a while, she realized that was all she was doing: glaring at her work. This was not what she'd imagined when she invited Cora to work with them. "Do you want to be working right now? You can leave. I can do this on my own," Nicole said.

"No, no, I do want to work on this," Ivan said.

Cora said nothing, so Nicole snapped at her: "Cora, could you please work somewhere else?"

Suddenly, Cora straightened up, looking all seriousness. Her giggles gone. "You asked me to work with you."

"Yes, but you're not working."

"I don't recall having to log a time sheet with you."

It wasn't worth it. Nicole mindulared: "I can't handle my work anymore. Anyone want to take a break with me?"

NICOLE WORKED at night for the rest of the week, skipping out of the telepaths meals. She finished the work on her own, leaving the records out for Ivan to see. She scheduled an appointment for them with Pre. Osterio, and stopped by Ivan's room to make sure he knew. He was distant, formal.

At the appointment, Ivan didn't show up. So, without any other choice, Nicole presented their results alone, giving credit to Ivan wherever it was due. Pre. Osterio was impressed with the work, and Nicole left the admin offices wanting to celebrate.

"Anyone up for a field trip down to Da Vinci?" Nicole mindulared, thinking it'd be nice to get away from Wespirtech's steel and granite halls. She'd heard that Da Vinci was quite beautiful, and it was only a short flight away. Wespirtech orbited Da Vinci, looking down at the beautiful planet from the height of Da Vinci's largest moon.

After a few minutes, when no one replied, Nicole began to worry. "What's everyone up to?" she mindulared. "You're all too busy now for a break?"

"Hey," Cora's mindular voice suddenly said, "how about we all get together after Ivan's and my meeting with admin?"

"Okay," Nicole replied. "I can wait until then."

The other telepaths agreed as well, and Nicole headed back to her room, wondering why Ivan and Cora were meeting with admin together. Maybe they wanted to switch rooms. Trade their singles for a double. Nicole felt a little left out. If it were her, she'd have talked to her best friend about it first. Maybe she'd go talk to Anna.

ANNA WASN'T in her room. Einray wasn't in his room. Nicole couldn't seem to find anybody these days. "I know we're all gonna get together after Cora and Ivan's meeting with admin, but I'm at loose ends right now," Nicole mindulared. "Anybody else looking for someone to talk to?"

When no one replied, Nicole headed to her own room, feeling really ignored. She lay on her bed, staring at the ceiling. Suddenly, Anna's mindular voice echoed in her mind: "Has anybody heard from Nicole lately? I borrowed a book from her and want to return it."

"Anna?" Nicole mindulared, sitting up and perking up. "I'm in my room; you can bring it to me here."

"I guess I'll just hang on to it a while longer," Anna said.

"Anna? Did you hear me?" Nicole said. No reply. "Can anybody hear me?" No reply.

Great, Nicole thought. Her telechip was broken. No wonder no one was paying attention to her. Maybe she could catch Ivan and Cora on their way back from admin. On her way towards them, Cora mindulared that their meeting was through. Ivan's chemist friend mindulared back to ask how it had gone.

"Osterio loves our work, but..." Cora said, and Nicole stopped, outraged: Cora hadn't *done* any work.

Ivan interrupted, finishing the thought for Cora, "Nicole already reported it as her own."

"What?!" Nicole mindulared, angrily, forgetting that no one could hear her.

"What do you mean?" Anna said.

"You know how she'd hang around the lab with us," Cora answered. "She tried to pretend the work was hers. She was in to see Osterio this morning. I guess she was jealous of my being better at physics. And of my being with Ivan."

"What kind of play are you putting on here?!" Nicole

shouted, ineffectually, through her broken chip. Although, she had to admit that Cora and Ivan had a good story. All that the other scientists had seen was Cora and Ivan in the lab all day. None of them had seen *her* working late.

"You're kidding..." Anna said.

"That is so low," mindulared Einray.

The solar biologists nattered about how surprising it was, and Ivan's chemist friend said he wasn't surprised at all.

What surprised Nicole, even shocked her, was that none of them seemed to care whether she could hear the nasty things they said. Her guilt opened her up to any and all character attacks, and they all assumed her silence was an admission of guilt.

Then, Nicole realized: her broken telechip was no mistake. With a single mindular signal, properly encoded, Ivan could disable any telechip he wanted. Easily. From a distance. Without anyone knowing. It hadn't seemed important that he had that power. Until now.

Indignantly, Nicole added to the fray of mindular words: "I was *never* interested in Ivan."

Then the tide of condemnation overtook her. Nicole sat back on her bed. Stunned, she listened to them rip her apart.

She was a thief. A pretender. Never any good at physics. So taken with herself. Who did she think she was? Not a scientist. Not worth knowing. They wished they'd never met her.

Anna tried to be nice...but her charitable thoughts soon folded. It was a crime too awful to contend against: to steal another scientist's work...unthinkable. They all hated her.

"I'm sorry," Nicole mindulared, although she knew it would do no good.

~

WHEN THE ADMINS came for her, Nicole was still listening to the telepaths talk. It had been days, but Nicole couldn't bring herself to take her telechip out. The conversation of her old friends, laced with cruelty towards herself, held a morbid fascination.

None of the telepaths would acknowledge her anymore, but she could sit in the dining hall, at her own, empty table, watching them and listening to their mindular talk. It was not healthy. These people were not, had never been, her friends. Yet she could not stop listening to them.

Nicole went mildly with the admins when they came. She told Pre. Osterio the truth: Ivan had been working with her; it was her research, not Cora's; Cora and Ivan were the ones lying. Pre. Osterio, looking more severe than usual, didn't believe her. Nicole couldn't really blame her. It looked like Ivan had done a bang up job of changing the computer records around. More than that, one liar was more believable than two.

"I guess you'll be sending me away from Wespirtech," Nicole said, feeling a strange sense of relief.

"It looks that way," Pre. Osterio agreed. "We can't have a scientist who would take credit for another's work. The other scientists wouldn't stand for it." Nicole's face colored, but she didn't say anything. The decision had clearly already been made. "Michaelson, our newest admin," Pre. Osterio continued, "is just outside my office. He'll help you prepare to leave."

Michaelson turned out to be the admin who'd fallen for Nicole's invisible blaster stunt. He walked her through a bunch of paperwork, and arranged a flight for her to Da Vinci. Nicole wondered how many of Wespirtech's scientists never took the time to see Da Vinci. It was so easy to get wrapped up in everything Wespirtech, and forget about the rest of...well, anything else. Maybe she'd visit the Chuarian flower yards while on Da Vinci.

Nicole finished the paperwork and was left with the task of

packing up her room. As she was leaving for the residential side, Michaelson said: "Before you go, will you tell me how you did it? How you made the invisible blaster work?"

Nicole looked at him blankly, not caring enough to answer. She went back in time and imagined that the blaster really had worked. She imagined Cora and Ivan writhing in pain, for real, on the floor. Nicole smiled, and Michaelson interpreted her smile as a sign that she meant to keep her secrets. "All right," he said. "Don't tell me."

WHILE NICOLE PACKED, she listened to the solar biologists explain a new cell structure they'd found in a species of stellar fungi to Anna and Einray. Nicole was sad to leave the scientific wonders of Wespirtech behind. She was sad to lose her friends, although they were already lost to her. Not one of them had stood up for her. Perhaps she was better without such friends. Would she find better friends in the world outside of Wespirtech?

Nicole couldn't imagine finding a friend she cared about as much as she'd cared about Cora. Perhaps that was her mistake: caring too much. How much had she really known Cora? How long? A few months. They'd been best friends... But only for a few months. That's not so long.

Nicole was no longer surprised by how Ivan had acted. Clearly, Cora had twisted him around her little finger. Nicole remembered calling Ivan easygoing and a teddy bear; now she realized that was just a nice way of saying spineless and easy to manipulate. She hoped he'd be happy with Cora. She wished she wouldn't miss Cora... To miss a person who betrays you... Pathetic.

Nicole looked around her empty room. It hadn't been all that hard to pack. Everything she'd brought to Wespirtech fit in one bag, now slung over her shoulder...everything except the sea-bunny, who was now Cora's. Walking through the residential side halls, Nicole caught one last glimpse of the sea-bunny through Cora's open door.

There was one thing left to do, before leaving Wespirtech forever. Her last act, still to be performed. Nicole cut into the lab section on her way to the flight. She found a random engineering lab and scrabbled through drawers until she located it: a zacto-extricator.

She was ready.

"Goodbye," she mindulared, lifting the zacto-extricator, positioning its grip behind her head. In her mind, Cora and Anna were talking. Their voices were pleasant, friendly. They were becoming the friends Nicole had urged them to be...then, suddenly, they weren't.

Silence. True silence. No longer could she hear words in her mind to which she couldn't respond. Nicole felt free. Shaken, but free. Like a young plant, that had been held up by supports, but also constricted by them. Now she had to stand on her own. She could see why mindular telechips had been nothing more than a fad on Earth I. Horrible to experience such an intense intimacy without the investment of having to work for it...

Nicole left the labs and went to the ship that would fly her away. She took her seat, ready to leave for Da Vinci. She didn't know where she would go or what she would do on Da Vinci. She had no plans. Wholly discredited by the premier institution of scientific inquiry, Nicole would never research again. No respectable scientist would ever look at her work.

But there were opportunities, great opportunities, out there: outside of these steel and granite halls... Nicole would find them. The ship took off.

5

THE NEBULA WAS EMPTY

The nebula was empty. Cold. Proto-star matter, so many dust motes, drifted, dully refracting the light of nearby constellations. The dust motes didn't even swirl. There was nothing to disturb them into motion, except for the nebula beast herself. In earlier times, during her youth, she frolicked—expanding space here; squeezing tight there; watching the space debris splash about. She chased the dust motes between her many dimensions, but now she was too sad to make her own fun.

The beast let out a somnolent sigh and stretched her stiffening body, tired from inactivity.

Even then, the dust motes didn't move: she was stretching only in the fourth and seventh dimensions. When she settled back into her lonesome repose, the fourth dimension snapped directly back into place, but the seventh dimension jostled the third which got briefly tangled with the second. Then the dust motes moved, shifting out of space that had grown smaller and rushing into the newly empty space.

The beast watched the motes hopefully, but when she realized it was only herself who unsettled them, she sighed again.

UNCONSCIOUSNESS CAME to the nebula beast, in all her mega-dimensionality. Time being the hardest dimension for her, she let it drift away, settling comfortably into her many spatial dimensions.

Sleep took her so fully that she was piqued with irritation when a radio wave roused her from her drowse. It tickled her persistently in the sixth dimension.

"Is anyone out there?" the radio wave asked. The beast froze herself, like unto holding her breath, focusing entirely on the radio waves.

"We're running out of fuel," the broadcast continued. Now the beast could sense the source in the distance, flying toward her. A tiny object! Metal, shiny, reflecting the light of every star like nothing in the nebula could. It was so beautiful, the beast fell instantly in love.

"We don't have enough fuel to go around the nebula, and I don't have enough air to sit here and wait..." The beast didn't understand the language in the radio waves; she only knew their feeling against her, as she twisted around the sixth dimension to feel them better. "I'm going to fly into the nebula..." The broadcaster broke off with a choked gasp. "Oh, god, I don't want to. I've heard of what happens to ships that..."

The dimensional beast's excitement was mounting as the exquisite, delicate little craft approached her, all satisfyingly lumpy in the first three dimensions. A friend! A tiny friend to cherish.

"Look, if you're out there, if you can hear this, answer me!"

The ship plummeted closer to the nebula, almost within reach.

"Well, that settles it." The beast began shuffling herself among the eighth through tenth dimensions, readying herself to greet her new friend. The dust motes roiled in chaos. "Here's to the other side." And the broadcast ended, but the craft was now in reach.

THE BEAST EMBRACED THE SHIP, hugging it to her in all the dimensions she could. Then, expanding the first three dimensions around it, she sought to see if it would grow. Bigger, she could look at it, but the tiny craft seemed to lose its cohesion... Quickly, she smooshed those dimensions back, but it didn't return quite to its original form.

The beast withdrew herself and watched the ship. It didn't move any more. It didn't set off little blasters, adjusting course. And it didn't tickle her with radio waves. Perhaps it was only startled? With a little time, it would return to activity...

But, no. The tiny friend, gleaming in the dull nebula light, did not spring back to life.

The beast sighed, slowly admitting the unrequited nature of her love. She re-approached the ship and scuttled it to the center of the nebula, where it joined her collection. All her unrequited loves... Such fascinating objects, alive in three, six dimensions—until they approached her. And then no more.

THE BEAST WAS ALONE. The dust motes settled around the row of decrepit ships, one ship longer than before. The nebula was empty again.

6

OF BEHEMOTHS AND BUREAUCRATS

News spread like wildfire of the first successful sun garden. The sun was Hegula, hearth of a destitute system. Normally, I don't waste my time on mining colonies. There are plenty of systems with two, three, or more populated planets. Those systems can supply me with crowds for months. Mining systems are a different matter. I've been to systems where the miners close the mines, gather up their families, and take the day off to see a good show. That's it. They have a great time, believe me. They enjoy my starwhals more than anyone in a cosmopolitan system. From my perspective, though, it's hardly worth weeks in the dead space between stars.

For Hegula, I made an exception. Everyone I talked to ached to see a sun garden. The mere concept had been *futura mythos* since anyone could remember. Now, it was actual arable farmland. I wanted to see it. And my line of work allows me to travel. Of course, I took the practical route: the starwhals and I edged towards Hegula with stops at all the most affluent systems on the way. It wouldn't do to fly straight. I'd save little time and miss many opportunities.

I reached Hegula's nearest populated neighbor, more than two years after beginning my slow journey. I hadn't thought much of the sun garden during the interim. It was merely the guiding light I navigated by. Nonetheless, I began to grow excited. In weeks, I'd be there. I radioed ahead, and it was such a small system my message was patched straight through to the mayor. I left for the final flight (a short two week hop) with assurance that the citizens of the Hegula Hephaesta Mining Colony looked forward to my presence. I was also invited to tour the garden.

For the starwhals, arrival in the Hegula system was like our arrival anywhere else. They coasted alongside my ship through the cold of space. When we reached Hegula's asteroid belt, I released a cloud of astral microbial dust. The starwhals fed, filtering the microbes like whales filter plankton through their baleen.

I put on my jet-pack space suit and zipped among the asteroids, setting up the field transmitters. Once switched on, the transmitters broadcast an electric field strong enough to keep the starwhals contained. It's like a giant playpen: enough space for the starwhals to soar about and a few asteroids enclosed with them to keep the landscape interesting. It's purely a precaution. The starwhals are gentle beasts. They're well trained, and they've never shown the slightest interest in leaving. What would they eat in the empty space of a star system? Outside of their native nebulae, they need me to feed them.

Next I set up the tent where the audience would watch. I picked a medium asteroid (more the size of a mansion than a moon) and lashed my clear flexi-glass circus tent to it. I turned the algae pumps on and sealed them inside. The tent would inflate in plenty of time for the show.

Then I noticed another space-suited figure watching me. My in-suit radio found the right channel, and I had my first conversation with Hegula Hephaesta's mayor.

"You must be Rhea," he said. "I'm Mayor Blanchley. Your beasts... what are they called?"

"Starwhals."

"They're beautiful. Are you busy? Would you like a tour of the colony?"

I looked at the three black blubbered behemoths. They'd keep. I accepted Blanchley's offer.

He escorted me onto his own small ship. I left mine parked on an asteroid inside the starwhals' enclosure. His ship was smaller than mine—designed for in-system flight, rather than star-hopping.

I have to admit, the colony surprised me. Though backwater, it had a rustic charm. No sparkling spheres of ocean and mountain; no sprawling centers of culture, science, and art; just rugged rock, carved into good homes where good people can *live*.

In all, the colony spread over a hundred some asteroids. The largest few cradled entire cities, covering the surface and burrowing beneath. Smaller asteroids sported state parks, nurtured at great cost under atmospheric domes. The very smallest asteroids were private homes, belonging to Hegula Hephaesta's wealthiest citizens. All the asteroids were clustered close enough for easy travel among them. A small, well-knit community... yet large enough to keep me and the starwhals busy giving shows for a few weeks.

My tour ended with a look at one of the larger mining asteroids, a giant rock laced with valuable metal and minerals. This particular mine, Blanchley told me, was representative of the others. Most of it had been eaten away, leaving a half-moon husk of the original rock. Valueless crumbs floated around the husk, remainders of the half that waned. Blanchley and his colonists feared the day when all the valuable minerals were mined and shipped away. What would their colony feed on then? Only, with the new sun garden, they had new hope.

"It's too late to show you the gardens today... not for the gardens, but for me. Mayors need their rest, you know. Perhaps tomorrow? Oh, wait, you're performing tomorrow. Well, the day after, then. Or any day. Name the day. For now, though, do you need lodgings?"

"I live on my ship, but thank you."

"I suppose I'd best return you." Blanchley piloted his little ship back through the colony and into the uninhabited patch where my starwhals waited. "Do let me know when you're ready for your next tour. I'm dying to show the gardens off."

"I'll bet you are," I said as I pulled my space suit back over my normal clothes. "I'm sure they're impressive."

"Oh, very impressive. And the truth is that I'm hoping very much to impress you..."

"How do you mean?"

"I have ideas of what this colony might become when the mines are gone... Hopes, shall we say. An attraction like your starwhals... Well, they'd fit in nicely."

I laughed. "You want to make Heguala Hephaesta a tourist attraction!?"

Blanchley smiled the sheepish but winning smile that helps many young politicians get elected. "Just let me know."

"I will," I said. "But don't you forget to come see the show you're scheming to keep."

By show time the next morning, my circus tent filled with eager spectators. Blanchley moved among them in all his mayoral splendor speaking words of mayorly wisdom. His voice rose above the others, but the volume of every voice was climbing.

I waited in my space suit, among the starwhals, all of us hidden from sight in the shadow of an asteroid. The clamor of the crowd filled my ears, channeled through my suit's radio. At the magic moment, when expectation peaks and threatens to fall into impatience, I started the show.

Speakers pumped music into the tent and my starwhals pumped waste gases out of the tube organs under their fins. The two older, larger starwhals jetted away from me to my left and right. They accelerated to an incredible speed and whizzed around the tent asteroid. Hermes, a mere calf compared to the others, jetted straight towards the flexi-glass dome.

I loved the gasps as Hermes and I, my legs wrapped tight around the knobbed end of his tailfin, stopped, suddenly, within inches of the flexi-glass. Until the last moment, the crowd had been too busy watching Jojee and Trina circling to notice our head-on approach.

During a final, blaring fanfare, I dismounted Hermes and used my suit's jets to maneuver along the length of his body, bringing me closer to the tent. Jojee and Trina joined formation behind me, and eager faces watched our every move from behind the flexi-glass.

"How many children here," I asked the crowd, my voice transmitted through the speakers, "have wished that a puppy would follow them home?" Hands shot up all through the crowd. "How many of you have wished you could run away and join the circus?" A few adults raised their hands to that one, I was amused to notice. "Well, that's exactly what I've done. My name is Rhea, and I'd like to introduce you to the three largest puppies ever to follow someone home."

Jojee, Trina, and Hermes took turns spinning axially as I said their names. After that, I walked the crowd through the usual spiel. Hermes jetted about as I pointed to and described the different parts of his anatomy. The children love learning about the starwhals: how they use their tube organs to jet through space; how they pick up radio waves, to communicate, with their narwhal-like horns; and how I found them in the Kleidadoan nebula.

Then the real stars of the show take over. Hermes does flips and somersaults. Jojee and Trina propel small asteroids about with blasts from their tube organs. The effect is halfway between an airshow and an aquarium exhibit.

I wonder if the starwhals would seem so whale-like if it weren't for their name... Their bulbous forms do give off more of the impression of elephant seals. However, their intelligence combined with their eagerness to do tricks, win treats, and please people always brings back the idea of whales to me. I miss them.

I'm getting ahead of myself.

The show went well, and Blanchley met with me afterward. We arranged a time for my tour of the sun gardens, and he informed me of the local news. The Expansionist government was threatening to institute martial law on Hegula if the system didn't pay its taxes. I wasn't worried. If there was trouble, it would take weeks or months to come. I'd be safely away by then. Even so, the Expansionists are reasonable. Or so I thought.

Blanchley took me to the sun garden on his little ship. It was a two part journey, since his ship didn't have the necessary shielding to fly into and land on the sun. So, we switched to a properly shielded ferry on Mercury X, the scorched planet most closely orbiting Hegula. All the windows were specially polarized; a mere fraction of the ambient light made it through them to my eyes, yet it was enough to bathe me in a brighter light than I'd seen in years. The depths of space I fly through are known for being dark.

I hadn't realized what I was missing. I felt positively giddy from the sunlight as I stepped out of the ferry and onto... well... the surface of the sun. At least, it *felt* like standing on the surface of the sun.

Blanchley explained the technology on the ride over. I'll see what I can remember, but the real people to ask are those Wespirtech wizards. I'm constantly amazed by what they produce.

The idea behind the sun gardens is to bring heliotropes (which are most plants) as close as possible to what they love: sunlight. Since stars have no solid surface, the Wespirtech scientists behind all this had to invent one. Thus, they constructed a huge bubble from massive and exceptionally expensive solar force shields and radiation osmitters. The bubble floats on the sun's photosphere... or maybe it orbits just above the photosphere... I don't recall. From space, this moon-sized bubble is so dwarfed, it looks like a bead of sweat on the hot face of the sun.

The effect, on the inside, is amazing. Orangey light glared all around me. The very ground beneath me transmitted it, since the soil is a nutrient-rich, fiber-optic sand. The translucency let me imagine I was walking on water... or magma, because of the glow. With the night sky, overhead, peeping between the tangle of trees, it was enough to take my breath away. When I imagine Eden, since that day, I imagine *that*: a living ball of plants, branches, vines, and brush, infused with a solar glow.

"Ready to move in yet?" Blanchley asked, seeing I was awestruck.

"Sure. If I can have a house *here*. Your asteroid belt is a lot less appealing." I pulled my shoes off and felt the damp, glassy sand under my feet.

"The only people who live in the garden work in the garden," Blanchley said with a touch too much seriousness. "Also, tenancy is handled on a rotating basis. The sunlight is highly filtered, but the gardeners still get more exposure than is normal. Many of them come down with something akin to Seasonal Affective Disorder, only opposite."

I laughed. Okay, honestly, I giggled. I was using my toes to draw in the sand, and I don't even remember what was funny, but I thought it was hilarious. Blanchley told me I was a prime candidate for Inverse Seasonal Affective Disorder. I thought that was funny too, but I took the clue and sobered up. I didn't want to find my tour cut short by a doctor visit, and Blanchley wasn't showing much of a sense of humor.

A head gardener joined us and walked us away from the garden's edge and the hatch in the outer wall of the bubble, where the ferry docked. He talked of the plants we passed, almost all gengineered to take full advantage of their special home on the sun. Their leaves grow upside down—the majority of the chlorophyll on the bottom. It makes them look more vivid, greener than most plants.

Before long, the gardener's discourse came around to the subject of taxes: "Since the Expansionists installed this facility, they feel proprietary about its produce."

"What percentage do they ask? It couldn't take much from a place like this to feed your entire system..."

The gardener's face was graced by a prim smile. "No it wouldn't take much. Five percent would do."

"They want it all," Blanchley said.

"None of it for the people who tend it? They must offer to sell it at cost... before you ship it away?"

"They pay the gardeners nominal salaries. Technically the entire installation is government owned, and they want all the produce shipped to Crossroads station for distribution to impoverished colonies."

"So, I work with fresh fruits and vegetables all day," the gardener added, "but my sons eat freeze-dried foods shipped from two systems away."

I was aghast. I couldn't imagine living in a small mining system, suddenly blessed with such bounty, only to watch the harvest reaped away. "No wonder you won't pay your taxes."

The gardener looked grim and Blanchley looked uncomfortable. If I'd questioned them further at the time... But it's no use going down that road. What's done is done. For the rest of the tour, we stayed away from politics, and I didn't learn about the Expansionist militia's imminent arrival until a week later when Blanchley's conscience finally got to him.

He sought me out in the starwhal's playpen. We were training, working up new tricks for the show. Blanchley watched and flattered us, chitchatting for some time before he told me. The Expansionists had decided to make an example of Hegula Hephaesta. If the first sun garden wrangled a deal, it would set a precedent. All the sun gardens would insist on keeping a percentage share.

That couldn't be allowed. So, a fleet of tanker ships, equipped with the latest beta-test drive from Wespirtech had been dispatched. With the new drive, they could arrive in days, rather than weeks. In fact, Blanchley was there to tell me, "The ships are already here. We're not giving in. We're making a stand. I'd have told you earlier…"

"But you thought they'd stand down."

Again, that sheepish grin. "I'm sure they'll let you go. We'll radio them, tell them you're not involved."

"I guess I'll start packing."

I wondered if Hegula Hephaesta had the firepower to stand up to the government. I wondered if the government would really have the nerve to attack them. I didn't wonder if the fleet would let me go, and it turns out that's what I should have worried about.

The starwhals and I made it to the edge of the system. One of the tankers intercepted us and fired a warning shot, accompanied by the radio signal, "No ships are to leave the system until the government's dues are paid."

"I'm not from this system!" I argued ineffectually against radio silence. My starwhals and I had no alternative but to return to the asteroid belt, where we'd been living. The starwhals were clearly shaken up by the warning shot, so I calmed them with a meal of mutated microbial dust that I save as a special treat.

I waited on my ship, watching through the windows. I imagined I could see dim flashes in the distance. Explosions? Weapon fire? Poor eyesight? Angered by my mistreatment and dazzled, still, by the Shangri-La I'd visited, I rooted for the Hegulans. Sure, I wished Blanchley had given me more warning... enough to get away... But the Expansionist fleet's behavior was beyond reckoning.

After a day of waiting and stewing, I risked the flight into the hub of Hephaesta colony. What I saw shook me to the very core: damaged, burning buildings; punctured atmospheric domes; scorched earth and shattered rock.

True, most of the asteroids were intact. Much remained undamaged. But, this was a small comfort, like a battered woman explaining that her abusive lover never broke her bones. Even one bruise is too many.

When I found Blanchley, I offered him the services of my ship. "It's not much, barely armed, but it looks like you could use all the help you can get."

Blanchley's eyes looked hollow. "We've surrendered, Rhea."

"When?!"

"Three hours after they opened fire."

"But, I saw explosions, still happening, minutes ago."

"They won't acknowledge our signals."

We stood in silence. What could either of us say? To believe we lived under a government *that* power crazy... It should have been unthinkable, but there was evidence, right in front of us.

"How is the colony faring?" I asked.

I could see the struggle on Blanchley's face. Should he tell the depressing truth or the optimistic, mayorly line? "We've got defense networks on our city-stroids, designed to deflect small asteroids. They work on the government missiles, too. Sometimes. Everyone's being relocated. Our mining ships are useless... We tried fighting with them, but we're just too slow."

Blanchley stumbled. "Our defenses will hold out. Not indefinitely. But they'll hold out."

The question, floating between us, was: when does the fleet plan to stop? Neither of us dared ask, and neither of us had an answer.

"I wish there was something I could do," I said.

"There is one thing: your starwhals... I'm worried about them."

I was confused. "That's kind but... aren't your people more important? A more pressing concern?"

"Yes, they are. That's why I'm worried. What would your starwhals do if the fleet shot down your force fields?"

"They're gentle, harmless animals..."

"Even when they're frightened? Have you ever seen them frightened?"

The warning shot from the fleet came back to me. It had *scared* them, but they weren't dangerous.

"Can you guarantee me that if they got free—rattled by explosions, pushed to the edge of terror, possibly injured—that they wouldn't do anything to harm this colony? They're large animals, Rhea. They could crush buildings, kill people."

My face burned with anger and shame. I couldn't promise him that. How could I? But... what he was asking... what I knew he was asking... it was too much. Too, too much. "I love my starwhals." He didn't have to tell me that a lot of people had lost *people* they loved. I knew it without him telling me.

That night, I lay on my bunk, in my ship. I tuned the ship radio to pick up the starwhals' song. It blasted over the speakers, and I sank into it. Those haunting voices, not meant for human ears, were so familiar to me. I imagined I could tell them apart: Hermes' voice high and playful; Jojee's a deep, reprimanding baritone; and Trina, good Trina, always reconciling the two.

When their dinnertime came, I fell asleep crying. I'd feed

them in the morning, I told myself. What Blanchley asked was wrong, but I couldn't get the picture he'd painted out of my head. My gentle giants, innocent nebula dwellers, on a horrible, deathly rampage. The truth was: I didn't know another way to kill them, and I couldn't take the risk.

Every mealtime, I reminded myself of the children who'd come to the shows. I imagined those same children, screaming in horror as the massy bulk of Jojee thrashed against Hephaestan buildings. Or, Trina's spear-like horn punctured the last, structurally sound, atmospheric dome. I hated seeing them as monsters, and it all melted away when they'd perform their tricks, hoping for treats. They begged for food in the only way they knew how, in the way I'd taught them.

Hermes arranged minor asteroids into loops, and jetted agilely through the self-made obstacle course. Trina and Jojee spiraled around each other, and passed asteroids back and forth on their jet streams like racquet balls. I could see the tricks getting harder for them, as they grew weaker. Trina was stronger than the others, and tried to help them. She nudged her body against Hermes, rousing him, urging him to go on. She did her routines with Jojee, covering Jojee's weariness and hunger born mistakes. Good Trina.

Each day, the three moved a little less, sang a little less, looked one step closer to death.

Maybe, if only, the fleet had left me alone for one damnable day, I would have given in and fed them. Instead, I found myself chasing away tanker ships, hoping I could keep them away until the starwhals died. I hoped for them to die! Just die fast enough, I said to myself. Die before I can't chase the ships away, and they set you free.

God, how I hate myself.

Blanchley came to me, in my mourning. He came onto my ship and told me the war was over. I could leave.

"What happened?" I asked.

"The fleet wasn't operating under government orders. The prototype drives malfunctioned, and flooded the ships with radiation. The officers knew they were dying, and that they'd sacrificed their lives to make an example of us."

"So, that's what they did."

"Yes," he continued. "The government ordered them to stand down when we surrendered. In fact, they weren't supposed to open fire on the asteroids at all. Just place us under siege, and shoot any ships flying between asteroids, or between the asteroids and the sun."

"Sounds more like the government I know."

"Yes," Blanchley agreed. After a pause, he said, "The ships stopped dead when their crews died. The Expansionist headquarters at Crossroads station wants to make a deal about the taxes now. In light of what's happened here."

I forced a smile, but I don't think it came out as one. Blanchley didn't ask about the starwhals, and I didn't tell him. He could see the lifeless bodies as well as I. He left, pressing me to stay or visit again. *That's* likely.

If they'd held on a few more days, we would have left together, my starwhals and I. We'd have taken our show back on the road, and I'd have never looked back at that hate-able system.

Maybe, I would have returned them to the Kleidadoan nebula instead. Yes, I would take them home. I'd never see them again, but I'd know they were alive. And well. Cavorting in their native plane.

Instead, I towed my starwhals to the sun that had been their undoing. I watched them fall, under the slow force of gravity, toward the ball of churning fire. I'd done the right thing. I tell myself, still, that I did the right thing. It would have been selfish to risk the lives of children.

The lives I mourn may have been the least of those lost for the Hegulan cause, but they were *mine* to look after. Jojee,

Trina, and Hermes *chose* to follow me out of their nebula, and I didn't ask for that responsibility. But I accepted it. They had no share in the events leading up to their demise; and, I take no share in the bitter-sweetness of the Hegulan victory. I cannot help but feel, I served my starwhals poorly.

The fire swallowed their dark bodies; I wish it had swallowed my pain.

7

______

DAISY CHAINING

Daisy chains are kind of tricky, so I didn't believe the frezzipod when he said he could daisy chain his way from Altu 7 to Altu 5 in fifteen minutes flat. First of all, that's a forty minute flight, if you pull up above the belt and fly without all those rocks in your way. Secondly, frezzipods look like a cross between a crab and a pineapple—the perfect tropical hors d'oeuvre. Who's going to believe anything a walking hors d'oeuvre says anyway?

So, I laughed at him. Big deal. Everyone laughs at frezzipods. The way they clatter around, those six arthropoidal legs, and that ridiculous bushy, green tail swinging from side to side behind them... That's just downright funny.

But then I made a mistake. "Yeah? Well, I could do it in *ten* minutes if I had one of those space convertibles like you drive." My buddies were laughing and jeering with me, but then it turned out the frezzipod had buddies too. One of his buddies offered to lend me a ship. Suddenly, my buddies weren't laughing anymore.

You'd think there'd be a way to back down. I mean, a human can't drive a space convertible without wearing a goddamn spacesuit for chrissake! Frezzipods can take the vacuum for hours, and convertible controls are designed for their clackety claw-hands. Me, though? I found myself sitting in a spaceship that hardly deserves the name—more of a space skateboard with an over-clocked engine, if you ask me— wearing a big, fitted bag of Kevlar, Mylar, whatever-*lar*-stuff.

My opponent's buddy, the other frezzipod, gave me a crash course in the controls, but I only had a few minutes to warm up before I found myself pushing full throttle on an alien space- craft, racing like my life depended on it for Altu 5.

Caddy, for that's what I'd decided to call my frezzipod *friend*, started the race with some extra-fancy moves. For a moment, I thought I was off the hook. Caddy headed straight toward a starwhal sized asteroid, before we'd even passed the start line, way too fast to dodge it. At the last second, Caddy sprang his six legs, jumping clear off his convertible.

My elation at having already won was followed fast on its heels by realizing what I was truly up against. Having sprung eight feet from his ship, and, conversely having pushed his ship eight feet in the opposite direction—a good, fat starwhal's girth —Caddy and ship sailed smoothly on. The asteroid passed *between* them.

I, on the other hand, took the slow way around, adjusting acceleration from one direction, then the other, canceling my spurious sideways motion out. When I got past the behemoth of a rock, I saw Caddy pulling himself and his ship back together via his safety tether, still sailing straight ahead.

I'm good, but Caddy was flying at a whole different level. And after a couple more tricks like that one—tricks I knew better than to try in my baggy suit with no prior experience—I was almost convinced Caddy could do it. He was way ahead of me. Maybe he really could daisy chain from Altu 7 to Altu 5 in fifteen minutes.

Then Caddy made his mistake.

See, he underestimated how fast I could dodge those rocks, daisy chaining the old-fashioned, sitting-in-my-ship-the-whole-time way. So, he was still close enough for me to see him when he ducked off planet-bound.

We'd used up eleven and a half of our minutes. I'd already been proved a liar, and in another four and a half—make that four—minutes more, Caddy would be proved a liar too. Except, it looked like he didn't plan on being there to get laughed at.

Well, to Jupiter with that! If I was going to be humiliated, the one thing that might help me save face was making sure Caddy got humiliated *more*. I hung a hard right, heading planet-bound too.

Not far off of the beaten trail, Caddy slowed way down. He had his ship moving at a virtual crawl, and he started doing something strange. The asteroids were thicker here, and when the small rocks—ones that wouldn't even knick your hull—hit his ship, Caddy carefully stopped to knock them back into place. He was covering his trail. Caddy had something to hide.

Well, he was going to be surprised when his hiding place turned out to be not so hidden. I was all steeled to confront that boastful, cowardly frezzipod and drag him back to Altu 5 the long, slow way when

~

HIS SHIP VANISHED.

~

I WAS FURIOUS. Had I blacked out? I've been flying the belt since I was a tween, and I'd never blacked out before. How else could his ship be there one second and not the next? How long had I blacked out for? I looked down at the timer on the convertible's dash. Just over fourteen minutes. I was still puzzling over it when

~

MY BUDDIES all started cheering for me over the radio. "Come on! You can do it!" they cried, snapping me back to the here and now.

The 'now' was fourteen minutes and forty seconds. The 'here'—I looked around, trying to orient myself—the 'here' turned out to be about four daisies from Altu 5. So, I pushed that little ship into gear, and I loop de loop de loop de looped around those last four asteroids...

Arriving at Altu 5, according to the automated ship-register, just in time.

Just in time to tie Caddy.

Holy Helios! I'd just daisy chained from Altu 7 to Altu 5 in fifteen minutes flat! Except, of course, I hadn't actually daisy chained the whole way. Neither had Caddy.

I took my time parking the borrowed convertible and suiting down. By the time I joined Caddy in the ship port bar, there were only a few minutes until my buddies, who'd taken the long way here, would arrive.

I wasn't sure how this was going to play out, so I took the stool next to Caddy's and ordered a marzicran sherry from the Canilon bartender. Caddy looked at me appraisingly over his drink. At least, I assume that's what the look on his pineapple-rind face meant. I know I was trying to appraise him.

"My *friend* and I here," he said, clackingly to the Canilon, "just daisy chained all the way here from Altu 7 in fifteen minutes." Caddy turned his myriad eyes back to me fixing me with a level stare. "*Flat.*"

"Is that so?" the Canilon asked, mixing my drink with his prehensile nose.

"Well..." I said, uncertainly, still trying to figure out the rules of the game we were playing. The Canilon shoved my finished drink toward me, looking skeptical. Caddy still had his eyes fixed on me, waiting to see what I would do.

If I called Caddy on cheating when he flew through that wormhole, he'd discredit me for not living up to my boast. For sure. I downed a big gulp of sherry and said, "Yeah, that's right. Fifteen minutes flat."

Caddy slapped me genially on the back with a crustaceous claw. At the same time, I heard my buddies approaching, raucously clamoring to hear about our race.

"You know," the Canilon said before they got to us, his lips curling to the side of his elephantine proboscis. "I can cut a cloverleaf around the Soris 'roids. *Without* stopping to refuel."

Now, that's clearly impossible.

Yet... No nose-handed Canilon ever cut a cloverleaf better than me. My buddies arrived just in time to hear me telling that elephant-face, "You think that's good? I can do it on *half* a tank!"

8

THE FAITHLESS, THE TENTACLED, AND THE LIGHT

The space-cruiser *Hypercube* glided into the Crossroads' station docking clamps with all the showy elegance that a ship of its price should have. Nicole Merison, the pilot, owner, and sole occupant of the *Hypercube*, shut the ship's engines down and put the rest of its operations on standby. With the ship safely locked down, Nicole grabbed a space-compression bag and headed off to enjoy Crossroads' atmosphere and markets. She'd been in deep space a long time, and, though she enjoyed the solitude, she was looking forward to the station's hustle and bustle.

Nicole's first stop was at her favorite food kiosk, where she ordered a spicy Golan wrap and asked after the local news. The proprietor, a short, stout alien with a pug face, told a story, probably a tall tale, about an entire alien civilization appearing, almost instantly, on an asteroid a few star systems away.

"Sure thing, Bauro," Nicole said, "when I start believing stories like that, I'll start accepting jobs from the government at their base pay rate."

Bauro laughed and said he didn't know why a nice girl like her took jobs with the government anyway. Nicole shrugged and pointed out that it was a government job that paid for her ship. She enjoyed her outlandish lifestyle, even if it did mean occasional freelancing for the Expansionists.

Moving on, Nicole stopped at a few fruit stands and picked up some choice pieces, fresh from the sun gardens of Zeta'ini III. She kept the fruit, along with a few other finds, in the space-compression bag flung over her shoulder. Then, Nicole headed for the station's communication center to check for messages. She was halfway hoping there wouldn't be any... She needed the work, after spending all her savings on the *Hypercube*, but that didn't mean she was looking forward to it.

Fortunately and unfortunately, Nicole found a message from the Department of Coordination for External Operators (DCEO) waiting for her. She considered ignoring the note; she had enough liquid assets left to get by for a while. Maybe, though, the mission would be interesting. The message did say to report to Prefect Galvin, her usual contact, immediately. Nicole decided to play along and headed for the government offices in the center of the station.

Most of the government offices were housed behind large, curving, plexi-glass windows. The DCEO was no exception, and as Nicole walked past Pre. Galvin's office, she tapped her hand, in time with her step, on the window. Pre. Galvin, a large woman, with black hair, and dark skin, looked annoyed. She always looked annoyed around Nicole Merison, so it was the only way Nicole had seen her. Nicole couldn't imagine working behind those huge windows: too much like living in a fishbowl.

"Hi, Nicole," Pre. Galvin said, as Nicole stood in her office's open doorway. "Do you tap on all the windows in this section? Or do you save that honor for me?"

"Just you," Nicole said.

"That's probably wise. You might get yourself kicked out the other way," Pre. Galvin narrowed her eyes, "and if you weren't allowed in the government sections, you couldn't work for us anymore."

"A huge loss for me," Nicole said, sitting down in the chair across the desk from Pre. Galvin. "What's the job?"

"You're staying then?" Pre. Galvin asked in her deep, rumble of a voice. "Lucky for me." Then, keying a code into her desk panel, Pre. Galvin called up an image of the Banti'phi asteroid field, a few star systems away. "Recognize this?" she asked.

"Sure," Nicole answered, "cruisers like me play around there all the time."

"Right. Which is why it was a cruiser like you who first found this..." Pre. Galvin zoomed the image in on one of the larger asteroids, and a series of tall, metallic, cylindrical buildings with bridges between them became visible on the asteroid's surface.

Nicole raised her eyebrows and waited, realizing there might be more to some tall tales than she'd expected.

"As far as we can tell," Pre. Galvin said, "these structures were all built during a period of less than a month. We sent a diplomatic team in to investigate and to get in touch with whoever built them. But something went wrong..." Pre. Galvin paused for a moment. "Our diplomat was returned unceremoniously to his ship and sent away... but they kept our scientist."

"*Your* scientist?" Nicole asked, hoping the answer was yes.

"She's from Wespirtech actually: Ms. Cora des Luz."

Nicole closed her eyes: Cora and Wespirtech. Those were the last two names she wanted to hear. She never said them, if she could avoid it, herself. They were names she was trying to forget.

"The job we're offering you," Pre. Galvin continued, "is to go in there, find Ms. des Luz, and get her out, with a minimum of trouble."

"What if I go in there, shoot... Cora, and say the crazy aliens did it before I found her, instead?" Nicole asked. Pre. Galvin didn't look amused. "You know about my history with her, right?"

"Your history together doesn't matter," Pre. Galvin said. "You like freelancing for the government, and we're offering you a freelance job suited to your talents. Fifteen thousand electro-marks on completion and five thousand as a down payment." Pre. Galvin didn't even have to address Nicole's threat to shoot Cora: the Expansionist government had Nicole's personality profile, and they knew she wouldn't go through with something like that. Nicole, for all her flare, was a good girl.

Nicole sat for a moment, remembering her time at Wespirtech. Remembering was disturbingly easy. She hadn't forgotten as well as she'd hoped. "Tell me about the aliens," Nicole finally said.

"They're cephalopoids, with nine appendages, all tentacular. They don't seem to communicate verbally. And they didn't like something that Ms. des Luz did... only we don't know what, because our diplomat was in another room. That's all we know."

Nicole could understand not liking Cora des Luz... these aliens might have a lot in common with her. "All right," she said. "I'll take the job."

"Just like that? I've never known you not to haggle..."

"I've never known you to offer me a fee that's equal to what a job's really worth," Nicole countered, but, deep down, she knew she wasn't doing it for the money. She just wished she knew what she *was* doing it for. All she did know, at that moment, was that there are some jobs you don't haggle over.

NICOLE SET her ship on autopilot for the trip from Crossroads to the Banti'phi asteroid field. She meant to use the free time studying up on all the Expansionist records of cephalopoid races... only, there wasn't much to study. The Human Expansion hadn't run into many sentient, cephalopoid races. Most of the information available was limited to studies of Earth I's base animals: squids, octopi, cuttlefish, etc. It wasn't much to go on, so, without that to occupy her mind, Nicole ended up thinking about Cora, instead.

What could Cora have done to upset a cephalopoid race? If they didn't talk, they wouldn't be bothered by her tone of voice, or the self-righteous things she said. And, Nicole didn't see how Cora could have done to them what she'd done to her. Suddenly, Nicole imagined Cora lying on a cold floor, beaten by slimy aliens. That was a good image. She wondered if that was why she had taken the job: a chance to see Cora at her lowest.

The *Hypercube* beeped at her, pulling Nicole out of her reverie. The autopilot part of the flight was over; she'd arrived at the asteroid field. This part of the flight was *made* for cruiser ships like hers to show off their moves: ducking and dipping between the asteroids. It was why the Banti'phi asteroid field was so popular among cruisers: no one around to object to their antics, and plenty of obstacles with decent gravity fields to sling shot among. At least, no one had been around to object before...

Arriving at the asteroid she sought, Nicole pulled the *Hypercube* into a long, slow arc, giving her a chance to get a good look. The cylindrical buildings looked about like they had on Pre. Galvin's screen. Nicole picked a likely outcropping of rocks near them, riddled with caves, to hide her ship in, and flew in for the landing. So far so good.

With the ship landed, Nicole looked out the windows, across the rocky, barren, surface to those alien buildings, stretched into the night-black sky. Nicole shuddered. She had her reservations about working for the government, but she loved the excitement of the jobs they found her. It was better than the stuffy research done at Wespirtech. Maybe she owed Cora a debt of gratitude for bringing her first career to its sudden end. If so, she didn't feel it.

Nicole dressed herself for her stroll across the asteroid in a loose fitting, all-purpose, gray jumpsuit. She'd paid plenty for it, but it was the only comfortable space suit she'd ever found. The seams around the neck, wrists, and ankles sealed right into space helmet, gloves, and shoes. When those weren't attached, it could be worn like any other jump suit. A new algae pack in the back of the helmet would keep Nicole good for air for several days... but, god, she hoped this mission wouldn't take that long.

Finally, Nicole grabbed an extra, less expensive, and less comfortable space suit, along with her standard tools to shove in her space-compression bag. If she did find Cora alive, she'd bet anything Cora wouldn't be wearing a space suit. Nicole rolled her eyes. Cora always was the type needing to be saved. Although, Cora would certainly have denied it if anyone ever told her so.

Once the *Hypercube* was locked down, Nicole made a beeline for the alien buildings and didn't bother looking for a door. She had the tools to make one: a high energy laser knife and a flexi-glass bubble.

Nicole pulled the flexi-glass bubble around herself, facing its opening to the cylindrical building's outer wall. Inside the bubble, Nicole had to crouch down; it was just big enough to hold her that way. Then, she pulled off the tape covering the sticky edge around the bubble's mouth. She pressed the mouth firmly against the building's outer wall, and the bubble sealed in place, ready to hold whatever atmosphere might be inside.

Nicole cut her entry with the laser knife, and, once the atmosphere equalized, she carefully shoved the plate into the building ahead of her. Her hand-scanner told her the atmosphere was good, so she took off her helmet and gloves, shoved them into the space-compression bag on her back.

Inside the building, Nicole replaced the metal panel in the wall behind her, hiding her homemade entryway. The map that came up on her echo-infra-meter's screen showed the building to follow this general plan: the perimeter of the building was a thick toroid, laced with winding, cramped passageways much like the one Nicole was now crouched in; the center of the building opened up into a large hollow area, cylindrical like the outside of the building. Most of the infrared occurrences were in rounded rooms nestled among the winding corridors.

Then, crossing her fingers, Nicole scanned for the characteristic radio wave transmitted by the tiny implant she knew Cora must have. The Expansionist government used those implants in all of its official personnel sent on dangerous missions. Of course, they only worked when the operatives remembered to turn them on and when they weren't being held in shielded areas. Fortunately, luck was with Nicole today. Cora was too optimistic about her own importance, and therefore certain rescue, to forget to turn on the transmitter. She was being held near the top of the building.

Nicole spent a moment weighing her odds in a wide-open space with few aliens against her odds in a mazelike series of closed in spaces with lots of aliens. She decided to bet on the wide-open space and headed towards the center of the building. At the very least, Nicole intended to see what the wide-open area looked like. She didn't take these jobs just for the money; half the fun was exploring strange and forbidden alien civilizations. That was her specialty.

As Nicole followed the passages towards the center of the building, she took a detour to see one of the larger, rounded rooms. Nicole approached the room and could see white light spilling out of its opening, into the darker hallway. Once inside, Nicole found that the light emanated from panels in the walls.

The light flashed and played around the curving wall of the room like the flickering lights on a Christmas tree. There were no buttons, switches, dials, or any other obvious kinds of controls—the panels of dancing light were perfectly smooth.

Nicole reached out to touch a panel and caught her breath as the room went dark. Then, point-by-point, the light returned, tracing out the shape her hand made on the wall. Curious. Nicole wanted to learn more about the lights... were they part of a computer somehow? or merely decorative? But she knew she had to move on.

With a growing desire to see the elusive cephalopoids, Nicole approached the end of the tunnel leading to the giant, open, room at the center of the building. She cautiously looked out of the opening and caught her first glimpse of the aliens.

The huge, stories-high, cylindrical space before her was laced with long straight poles, stretching from floor to ceiling and occasionally from wall to wall, across the giant room's diameter. The one, curving wall that defined the space was riddled with openings to tunnels like her own. It was a strange structure.

Yet, the building's structure was oddly suited to the tentacled creatures, much like Earth I's octopi, Nicole saw moving in their strange, complicated dance before her. Nicole pulled out a mini-magolucar to get a closer look.

Nicole zoomed the magocular's view in on a cephalopoid crawling out of a hole, across the building from her. Its tentacles, which numbered nine, were gray and curvaceous. They grew radially out from the base of the cephalopoid's oblong, sack-like body. Where tentacles and body met, the cephalopoid's yellow and intense eyes were set. There was nothing resembling a face, but the stretched skin around the eyes, and the eyes themselves, were extremely expressive. The alien looked suspicious, alert, interested. Nicole was intrigued.

Where had these aliens and their buildings come from? Why were they here?

Nicole watched as the cephalopoid deftly maneuvered itself away from the tunnel entrance and across the large room, by way of the light gravity and the many long poles. Long tentacles reached to one pole, grasping with the underside of sucker-disks, as other tentacles lightly let go of the last pole. With nine tentacles, there were always enough. The cephalopoid was a gracefully and efficiently built creature, and its motion showed it. Nicole was suitably impressed. She knew she would find climbing the poles to the top of the building much harder. Still, it was time to try.

Rifling through her backpack, Nicole located two of the most useful devices she always carried: a light grenade and an ultra-dark. The ultra-dark was an eye patch, meant for people who had trouble sleeping. It was extremely effective at blocking unwanted light. The light grenade was extremely effective at providing unwanted light... at least, light that was unwanted to anyone who *saw* it. Nicole always arranged not to see it, and she *definitely* wanted it.

With a deft swing of her arm, Nicole flung the live grenade high into the air. The low gravity gave it a long, graceful arch. In fact, Nicole had the ultra-dark safely over her eyes, before the grenade showed any proclivity for falling back down. Usually, Nicole knew when the grenade went off from the shrieks of pain it elicited. This time, the grenade's detonation was eerily silent. Nicole counted to ten and pulled off the ultra-dark.

At first, Nicole was afraid she'd killed them. The cephalopoids, who had all been shades of white to gray, were now as black as ash. They clung to the poles, shuddering. Blackened lumps of tentacles, wrapped around themselves in fright. It was their shuddering that allayed Nicole's fear: they were just shocked. Perfectly natural.

Knowing time was limited until the effect of the brilliant

flash wore off, Nicole jumped from the tunnel's mouth into the open space before her. She grabbed a pole and flung herself, hand over hand, upward, switching from pole to pole whenever convenient. Traversing the giant room in this manner, Nicole made it to the top, well before the cephalopoids could regain their sight.

She found a large opening, larger than the other tunnel entrances, at one side of the ceiling. From the echo-infra-meter's map, she knew it led to the area where Cora's signal came from. Nicole pulled herself into the opening, and cautiously followed the tunnel towards those rooms.

Nicole found herself in an area that felt much more normal to her than the confined tunnels and the giant, open room with the poles. These rooms at the top were more human sized, and they were filled with complicated machinery. Perhaps it was some kind of lab. The walls glittered with panels of flashing lights, like those she had seen before.

Nicole ducked behind a large tank filled with a luminous fluid as she noticed several cephalopoids working with the machinery at the far end of the room. Their tentacles moved rapidly, deftly. They seemed to be doing a dozen things at once. Nicole wondered how she'd fare in a hand to tentacle fight with one of them. They didn't look strong, but, then, their flowing bodies were probably ninety percent muscle. Not to mention that cephalopoids wouldn't have any bones to break.

Fortunately, these particular cephalopoids hadn't noticed her, and Nicole managed to work her way around the back of the large luminous tank, remaining unseen. She found herself in the short tunnel leading to the room holding Cora. She drew a deep breath. She knew there was only one infrared reading in the room... Yet, she would rather have faced a room filled with wrathful, slippery, and immensely muscled cephalopoids.

Nicole entered the room.

Cora was crouched in the far corner of the room, her arms wrapped around her knees, and her head leaned upon them. She looked asleep. She looked small. Nicole felt an ache in her heart for the hugs such a reunion might have involved if Cora had cared for her as she cared for Cora. Betrayal is hard to believe in: the mind rejects it, readier to forget a telling transgression than years of misinterpreted friendship.

Nicole made herself walk towards Cora and found herself stopped short by an invisible force field. She reached her hand out and felt it repelled as if her hand and the empty air were both magnets. Nicole pulled out her echo-infra-meter and discovered that the empty space before, in fact, appeared as a wall on her map.

Nicole spotted a control panel with actual buttons and examined it. After a little experimentation, she discovered the force field was easy to control from her side of the room.

It created an ionization field that manipulated the air in the room. So, the invisible force field was merely a sheet of highly, unnaturally densified air. If Nicole manipulated the field, only slightly, she could cause all the air in Cora's cell to be drawn into the wall... leaving Cora in a vacuum. Or, it would be just as easy to bend the field to fill Cora's cell entirely... air would whoosh past her to flood the little cell, making it all as dense as the wall. Cora would be crushed. It would be even easier than shooting Cora.

Nicole's hand hovered over the controls as she watched Cora sleep for a painfully long time. She imagined a million things to say to Cora. In her mind, she heard herself make accusations... threats... demands... Instead, she simply turned off the force field and stood there.

Eventually, Cora began to rouse. Groggily, she looked up. "You've come to save me?"

Nicole pressed her lips into a smile and nodded. She felt cowardly. She walked over to Cora, offered an arm, and helped her up. As a look of recognition crossed Cora's face, prickles ran down Nicole's neck. She wanted to tell Cora how easily she could have crushed her with the force field. All that came out was, "Have they been feeding you?"

Cora looked surprised. "Nothing I could eat," she answered.

Nicole pulled a nutrient bar out of her backpack and handed it to Cora. She refrained from commenting on Cora's finicky tastes. "Here," she said, "this will keep you going until we get out of here."

"You have a ship waiting?" Cora asked, hope in her eyes.

"Yes," Nicole said, eating up the look of those eyes she hadn't seen in so long. The last time she had seen them, they had looked so hardened and hateful. Cora would do the same again, Nicole reminded herself. Do not trust her. "Before we go, I want to find out what happened here. Why they locked you up..."

Cora shrugged, suddenly impatient. "They're crazy aliens. They probably wanted to experiment on me. *We should go.*"

"*Have* they experimented on you?" Nicole prompted.

"Well..." Cora began but didn't finish.

"Right, then that's probably *not* why."

"Well, but wait, I have been talking to their computers. I didn't have anything else to do... I'm sure they've been learning from that."

"Okay," Nicole said. "Show me."

In answer, Cora walked back into the part of the room that had been her cell and placed her hand against one of the wall panels. It lit up under her hand as the other panel had lit up under Nicole's hand earlier. Cora drew shapes with her index finger on the smooth panel, and words followed her finger, shining in a white light. "I just talk to the computers like this. They have very good machine learning algorithms. They might even be an artificial intelligence..." Cora looked up at Nicole. "Sometimes the computer spells things out too, but it doesn't make much sense yet."

"Hmmm," Nicole said. "I'm not convinced. They could have had you *and* the diplomat talk to the computers without locking one of you up. I still think you did something to upset the aliens."

Cora looked uncomfortable and voiced her distress in assertions of her outraged innocence.

"Look," Nicole said, "just because you upset them doesn't mean you did anything wrong. They're aliens; we don't know what might upset them." It felt weird assuaging the guilt of someone Nicole very much wanted to feel guilty. She sighed. "Just tell me what you did."

"I didn't know it would make them mad..." Cora said.

"I know," Nicole assured her, "just tell me."

"Okay," Cora consented. "Did you see the room with all the machinery?"

"Yeah, it's right out there," Nicole said beckoning to the tunnel she entered by.

"Is it? I guess they didn't take me very far... Anyway, there's a tank out there. It's filled with a glowing water."

"Yeah, I saw that," Nicole said.

"I thought it might be related to the computers... the glowing lights..."

"That makes sense," Nicole agreed.

"So, I took a sample. It was just a small sample. I just wanted to scan it." Cora's voice was speeding up as she spoke. "They weren't watching, I thought. They were talking to Gentry, the diplomat I came with. I didn't think they'd care. I just wanted to know what the computers were made of... But they came rushing at me... Their skin was flushed red... They'd looked so small and delicate, and suddenly they were so large... scary... wrapping their tentacles around me..." Cora's voice broke off entirely, as if it had sped up beyond the point where her mind could keep up with it.

Nicole put her hand on Cora's shoulder. "It's okay," she said, but her heart wasn't in the attempt at comfort. She was too absorbed in this new problem: were the computers made of something valuable? Something rare? Something dangerous?

"Nikki," Cora said, interrupting her thoughts, "can we go?"

Nicole frowned. No one called her *Nikki* anymore. She'd thought she missed it... apparently she'd been wrong. "You didn't get a chance to find out what they're made of?"

Cora shook her head, looking down, probably still absorbed in her memory of the cephalopoids attacking her. Nicole enjoyed that image... but, she pulled herself away from it, returning to logic problem before her.

Consumed in thought, Nicole walked over to the glossily smooth wall panel. As her shadow fell over the panel, Nicole thought she saw a slight sparkle fill the shape of her darkened silhouette. She placed her hand on the screen, and the screen glowed in response, as it had before.

Nicole hadn't yet decided what to do, and before she got the chance, she was startled by the glowing light spelling out the words "not Cora" in Cora's handwriting. Cora and Nicole looked at each other. When Nicole looked back, the lights had spelled out "who?", again in the only handwriting they knew.

"Has it talked to you like this before?" Nicole asked.

"I said it tried to a little..."

Nicole frowned. She had a hunch. "It would be easier if it could hear me..." she mumbled while tracing the shape of her own name on the panel, followed by a repeat of the question "who?" Of course, Nicole was not surprised when the panel sparkled archaically in response. She didn't expect it to have a name... but she did think it deserved one. "Let's go," she said to Cora, suddenly worried.

∿

THIS TIME, Nicole decided to keep to the tunnels, avoiding the central, cavernous room. She would have liked to move quickly, but her need to avoid cephalopoids limited her to moving stealthily. With her echo-infra-meter held before her, Nicole led Cora downward through the winding tunnels.

"We're going to your ship now?" Cora asked from behind, and her voice echoed through the tiny halls.

"Yes," Nicole answered without stopping, without turning her eyes away from the meter's map.

"What did I do wrong?" Cora persisted. "You're acting like you figured it out."

As Cora finished her question, Nicole's path-finding led them into one of the small rooms nestled among the tunnels. Panels lit up as they entered, swirling with light. Nicole led them away as quickly as she could.

"They're not computers," Nicole said, doggedly continuing through the tunnels. "They're not artificial intelligence. They're just intelligence, and I think you hurt them."

Nicole couldn't see Cora's face behind her, but Cora looked surprised, and then remorseful. For the last week, all she'd done was talk to the computers... rather, the living lights. She realized that she liked them. Cora and Nicole continued in silence the rest of the way.

When, finally, they reached the tunnel Nicole had entered by, she went straight for the panel she'd cut in the wall. She pulled a second flexi-glass bubble from her backpack, so that she and Cora could seal the one behind them before rupturing the first. She began to remove the metal panel in the wall... but was interrupted by a loud knock ringing out behind her.

Nicole and Cora both turned to see a cephalopoid, a single cephalopoid, in the hall behind them. One tentacle was raised, wrapped around a transparent bulb. Lights played fitfully inside the bulb. The rest of the cephalopoid's tentacles writhed, rhythmically, on the floor. It banged the bulb of light on the floor, and the knock rang out again.

Nicole was paying attention; Cora was hiding behind her.

The cephalopoid's eyes were focused, clearly, on the intruders. The pupils of its eyes were black bars, across the gold intensity of the irises. Nicole felt they were piercing through her. Then, abruptly, the intimidating demeanor of the cephalopoid changed. The black bars narrowed into lines, and the cephalopoid looked as if it were smiling, almost laughing. The change was subtle, yet ubiquitous; effected entirely by the eyes and a stretching of the skin around them. Nicole noticed light blues and yellows flushing the fleshy skin of the cephalopoid's tentacles.

"Did the diplomat manage to communicate with them at all?" Nicole asked Cora, who was shuddering behind her.

"Gentry?" Cora asked. "He..." but she trailed off as the answer appeared in two glowing letters: *NO*.

"You can hear us," Nicole said, now addressing the cephalopoid and the bulb of glowing light.

"Yes," glowed the bulb, as the cephalopoid writhed inscrutably, the blue and yellow blushes on its tentacles flitting erratically. "We weren't interested in talking to the others..." scrolled, brightly, across the bulb. "We *are* interested in you."

Nicole was confused. For one thing, she wasn't sure who she was talking to: the cephalopoid or the glowing bulb. For another, it was damned strange reading those words in Cora's handwriting. "I'm sorry," she said, "me? Why me?"

"You have style," the bulb glowed. "Sneaking in... Taking what you want... Learning what you want... We had no patience for the others."

"Who are you?" Nicole asked. "Where do you come from? Why are you here? And are you going to let us go?"

"We travel together," the bulb glowed. Then, after a darkened pause, the bulb beamed, entirely lit up. "The diatomes are shy..." were the words that followed the beam. "They write what I want to say," the bulb glowed cryptically.

"So, I'm talking to..." Nicole said, "the cephalopoid?"

"Yes," the bulb, or rather diatome, agreed.

"My other questions," Nicole urged. "Answer *them*."

"We travel between universes," the diatome glowed. "We'll be moving on soon."

"Will you let us go?" Nicole asked again, her curiosity overwhelmed by more pressing concerns: she worried that they might insist on keeping Cora.

"Nicole can go," the diatome glowed.

"What about my friend?" Nicole was too worried to notice her word's irony.

"You put a lot of work into rescuing your friend," the diatome glowed. "We find that interesting."

Nicole could feel Cora getting nervous, almost frantic behind her.

"She is dangerous. She hurt us."

"What would you do with her?"

Finally, the diatome glowed the following words: "We do not kill. Take her with you."

Nicole nodded. "Thank you," she said. After a long pause, Nicole decided they must be done with her. "I guess, we'll go now?"

"Wait," the diatome glowed. "One last thing... We leave soon..." The cephalopoid squirmed its tentacles discomfitingly. The diatome surged with light: "I want to stay."

"Who wants to stay?"

"ME. This diatome."

Cora stepped forward, "I'll take it," she said, hunger in her eyes.

"*NO*," the diatome glowed, "not Cora. *Nicole*."

Nicole laughed nervously. "Sure," she said.

The diatome swirled with shining light as Nicole reached out her hand. Before the cephalopoid passed the diatome from its grasping tentacle, its alien eyes caught Nicole's. She realized the trust she'd taken on.

As the cephalopoid retreated into the tunnel, the pupils of its eyes widened to black bars, and the blush left its tentacles, a fleshy, placid gray.

Nicole placed the diatome carefully in her space-compression bag, for the trip back to her ship. She exchanged a look with Cora and could see there would be no trouble over the diatome. Cora could make trouble, certainly, if she wanted. But, she was already building up her denial. She wouldn't mention the cephalopoids or diatomes again. So, the government need never know about it.

BACK ON THE *HYPERCUBE*, Nicole prepared her ship for the flight home to Crossroads station. As the engines powered up, she sensed Cora walk up behind her.

"I could get you your job back," Cora said.

Nicole closed her eyes and put her hand to her head. Not an apology for causing her to lose her job in the first place; not even a thanks for rescuing her; just an insincere offer.

"I really could," Cora continued. "I'd just tell them... I'd tell them what happened."

You mean, Nicole thought, *that you could finally tell the truth?* She tried to ignore Cora and get back to revving up the ship. Yet, she could feel her heart racing in spite of herself. To go back to Wespirtech...

"I'll do it if you ask," Cora said. "Even though it would mean losing my own job."

"Sure you would," Nicole said, finally nettled into responding.

"No, really," Cora continued. "Just ask."

Nicole thought about it. She knew Cora was lying, but somehow it didn't make her as angry as she thought it would. For all her idolization of those years at Wespirtech, it wasn't really the heaven she remembered. In fact, it had been quite the opposite: the worst hell she'd ever seen, and Nicole had seen the inside of quite a few alien dungeons, torture chambers, and prison cells. The difference was that angry aliens are honest about the horrible things they plan on doing to you. Nothing at Wespirtech had been what it seemed.

"Okay," Nicole said. "I'm asking. You go back there and tell them what really happened."

Suddenly, Cora was surprised. She clearly hadn't expected Nicole to be so uncouth as to take her up on the offer. "I will," she said. "I mean, I'll try. I don't know if they'll believe me now. It was so long ago. But I'll try," Cora finished, lying.

Nicole smiled. She knew now why she'd taken the job. It was time to move on, and she couldn't do that while still hating Cora; and she couldn't stop hating Cora while she still believed in their lost friendship. She had come to see Cora at her lowest. Only, Cora's lowest wasn't lying beaten on the floor of an alien cell; it was standing up on her rescuer's ship and lying through her teeth to the woman who'd saved her life.

Nicole looked at her new companion, the diatome resting on *Hypbercube's* dash. She wondered about all the places it had been. The diatome was beginning a new phase of its life, choosing to travel with her. Nicole supposed she was beginning a new phase too. She liked starting out together with this strange orb, happily singing in patterns of light.

$$9$$

THE GENETIC MENAGERIE

Brent Schweitzer was born on planet Da Vinci, the foremost center of knowledge and learning in the Human Expansion from Earth. The planet was lush and green, with deep blue rivers cut into its surface like veins of gem cut into stone. Warm in the summer, brilliant with fire work colors in both spring and fall, and temperate in the winter, Da Vinci was as idyllic as any of the worlds the Human Expansion had found. As such, Da Vinci was deemed the appropriate setting for the host of art schools and other centers of academia that began to grow there as naturally as the native flowers. For, without scenery, without inspiration, how can there be art and learning?

Brent Schweitzer, growing up on Da Vinci, enjoyed the natural splendors of his home. His parents took him camping every summer. Once, they took him half way around the world to the Chuarian Flower Yards, where flowers native to every planet in the Human Expansion are grown. Brent was enthralled, and as soon as they returned he started his very own flower collection. Brent's parents approved of his enthusiasm for aesthetics and soon began taking him to visit the many, fine colleges on their planet. Brent was a bright, sensitive, young boy, exactly the kind of student such universities sought.

Brent, however, had other ideas for himself. His eyes had long turned toward Da Vinci's moon, a barren world without even a name. What the moon did boast was The Western Spiral Arm Planetary Institute of Technology, better known as Wespirtech. Wespirtech had been founded with one goal: to be the single most powerful institute of scientific research in the known universe. It had long since succeeded at that goal.

Visible from Da Vinci on a good night, Wespirtech jutted out of the near side of the moon in an array of straight lines and boxy figures, as gray and dull as the surface of the moon itself. It didn't look much better closer up. Wespirtech's inhabitants rarely saw it from the outside, however, for it's architecturally uninteresting buildings were built directly in the vacuum of the moon's non-existent atmosphere. The buildings were connected by the occasional skybridge, but, mainly, they were connected by a rabbit warren of tunnels underground, which the research scientists called the Daedalus Complex.

What Wespirtech lacked in inspiration, it lacked in distractions as well: for a beautiful landscape may inspire an artist, but it's merely a distraction and a waste of time for a scientist. Or so the theory ran. The barren surroundings, however, did have their uses. For one, they made low gravity and vacuum based experiments easy, and they provided the perfect buffer against any experiments gone wrong. Wespirtech was naturally quarantined.

Brent Schweitzer first turned his eyes to Wespirtech, and away from Da Vinci's leading art colleges, when he learned that his favorite flower, a variant of the terran ghost orchid, had been genetically engineered on his homeworld's very own moon, at Wespirtech. Brent was good in school and popular among the teachers, so he found little trouble convincing the biology teacher to tutor him in genetics on the side.

By the time Brent sent his application to join the scientists at Wespirtech, he had begun his work on the Keats and had designed a cat whose fur changed color with its moods. The cat was a gift to his mother on her birthday with which both she and the admissions committee for Wespirtech were equally delighted. Although, even more intriguing to the admissions committee was Brent's work on the Keats. He had been increasing the memory, reasoning, and language capabilities of parrots (whose genetically evolved counterparts were drolly termed Keats by his mother) mainly to increase their desirability as companion animals. Wespirtech admissions, however, immediately saw the Keats' potential use as translators: hardwire a few languages into the Keats' memory and send one on the shoulder of every diplomat headed to a heated negotiations table. Wespirtech *must* have them, it was decided.

Since the rights to Brent's work came with Brent, his acceptance was dispatched at once. Brent's parents were a supportive pair, and, despite their early hopes that Brent would be an artist, they could not have been prouder when his acceptance came. Brent left his home on Da Vinci amid a veritable fanfare of hugs, tears, hopes, promises, and expectations. His parents wanted him to be happy, but industrious; to make new friends, but not forget to write; and above all to come home for Christmas. Brent promised everything. He even sincerely promised to miss them.

ALTHOUGH LACKING IN SCENERY, Wespirtech proved to have its fair share of distractions. For one, the scientists led an active night life of standard and live-action role-playing games (generally carried out in the winding corridors of the Daedalus

Complex), replete with the most complicated rules that the most technically adept human minds in the galaxy could construct. Furthermore, though it was kept quiet, a society solely composed of such creative and *experimental* minds, necessarily given access to whatever cutting edge technologies their hearts might desire, could not be kept entirely drug free. The administration's policy was to turn a blind eye as long as productivity wasn't affected and the resulting chemicals stayed *on* world. The scientists dabbling in drug creation for their own experimentation was one thing; dealing in them would be quite another.

In his first few years at Wespirtech, Brent tried each of the distractions it offered him, including the attentions of a young physicist named Anna. Although she was not especially pretty in the traditional sense, Anna's face lit up and her eyes sparkled when she talked about physics or advancements in technology. Her enthusiasm made her sufficiently attractive to captivate Brent for more than a few months and make Anna the subject of several of his letters home. In the end, however, Brent found Anna's failure to be interested by anything other than technology and physics tiresome, not to mention that he discovered his interest in the opposite sex in general to be less intense than he'd expected. Needless to say, Anna was disappointed in her aspirations to become Anna Schweitzer.

All in all, Brent finished his work on perfecting the Keats as translators in good time. The administration was impressed and began encouraging him to work on their pet project. At the administration's and his colleagues' urging, Brent began work on genetically increasing the human life span. His progress was promising. Everyone was thrilled, including Brent... at first.

∼

OFFICER CICERO PUT down the worn in, beaten up paperback he was reading and leaned back in his co-pilot's chair. He knew the story of Brent Schweitzer's early life by heart. He'd read the wildly successful biography by Gloria van Santen at least a hundred times. He'd dug up every one of the thirty odd interviews with Anna Karlingoff about her one time lover and colleague of many years. He'd done everything short of making the trip to visit Schweitzer's childhood home. That was probably for the best, however, since Schweitzer's parents let it be known that they were ready to be done with the press and the public only five years after the big day, the day it all happened.

Cicero twisted his chair around on it's swivel and chuckled to himself. Officer Hyland, who was piloting their space ship, looked over.

Catching Hyland's eye, Cicero started to speak what was on his mind: "He must have spent *years* planning his crime. Do you ever think of that?"

Hyland rolled his eyes. "I think of it all the time," he replied. "I think of it every time we start to approach a planet and you have to start talking about it again."

"Well, this planet could be the one!" Cicero replied with excitement. He looked hopefully at the image read out on their sensors the blue, green world hanging before them in space. "We need to be ready," he added soberly. "We need to be in the *mindset*."

"Mindset!?! There is no mindset, Cicero. We scan the planet; we see he's not there; we go on to the next planet."

"But this planet could be the one."

"*This* planet could be the one. The *last* planet could have been the one. Any old planet could be the one." Hyland threw up his hands in despair, and then added after a moment: "The *next* planet could be the one, you know, and we'd just be wasting our time on this one. Did *you* ever think of *that*?"

"We'll deal with that when we get there. *If* we get there.

Right now, I'm just trying to do my job and that involves taking this planet seriously. We could find him here."

"No," Hyland objected, deftly running a few scans in addition to verbally fencing with Cicero. "You're not just trying to do your job. You're trying to feed your obsession and solve the mystery. You *can't* solve the mystery. It's been analyzed from left and right, top and bottom, up and down."

Cicero frowned, and Hyland shook his head while perusing the scan readouts: all negative, no signs of the stolen spaceship. With a minor touch to the thrusters, Hyland shoved the ship into a different orbit and started the scans again. Then, muttering to himself, Hyland said: "Every person who ever knew the Great and Infamous Brent Schweitzer has been interviewed, and they all said the same thing: they don't know why he did it."

"That's not true," Cicero responded, to Hyland's immense irritation. "Anna Karlingoff had some very interesting theories about why he did it, and Schweitzer's mother wouldn't comment, which I take as a sure sign that she knew. Think about it. If he told anyone what he was up to, what he had in mind, it would have been his mother. They were very close. He gave that color changing cat to her."

Hyland glared at Cicero.

"Look, I wouldn't have volunteered for this job if I didn't care," Cicero defended himself. "You don't seem to care at all, so why did you volunteer?"

"I want to be a hero."

"Ah, the hero who brings Schweitzer and his long-life tonic back home. You should be even more eager to find him than I am."

Hyland abandoned his scans and swung his pilot's swivel chair around to look Cicero in the eye. "The difference is," he said, "that I don't care why he did it, as long as we bring him back. He stole valuable technological equipment from the

Human Expansion, including that damned prototype spaceship that let him get away so fast... not to mention stealing himself. Think of all the great work he could do... could have already done." Turning back to his planetary scans, Hyland added, "The men who bring him home will be written down in the history books, that's for sure."

Cicero chuckled again. "History books are one thing. I want Gloria van Santen to interview us for her sequel. She'll write a sequel, won't she? Her biography of him was so successful, you'd think she would anyway. What a writer. So insightful."

"So sensational."

"Yeah, but I like it," Cicero said. "She makes the story fun to read: all the tension and mystery of the night when he loaded up that ship... wondering if he'd be caught... how he'd carefully gathered all the right security codes by buddying up to his colleagues... and that final moment, when everything's ready, and he's about to take off... it's exciting. Schweitzer would probably enjoy it himself. We'll have to give him a copy to read on the way home in his cell."

Cicero fell into a reverie, imagining all the possible plans Brent Schweitzer might have had and what he'd have done with his thirty odd years of lead time, the time it took to build another ship fast enough to chase him and then the last few months spent planet hopping looking for him. He'd be an old man by now, growing older every day that they continued to search for him. "I hope he's not dead," Cicero thought to himself but out loud. "I'd like to get a chance to talk to him. Finding him dead would be the worst... what if he crash landed? We'd never know his plans... "

Hyland's mouth dropped open. "Oh my god... " he said. "That's it... that's the ship. He's here." Hyland turned to Cicero, joy and satisfied anticipation joined by a new anticipation washed over his face. "You're about to get a chance to find out."

~

HYLAND AWKWARDLY NOSED the space police ship down into the atmosphere, much as Brent Schweitzer had piloted his ship some thirty years before. Since both ships were prototypes of the new elasti-drive, neither had been designed to land on planets particularly well. Presumably, that feature would be added into later models. Mainly, the first ship had been built to test the new drive, a product of Anna Karlingoff's work, and the second ship had been built to catch the first.

Anna Karlingoff, following her brief but life-altering affair with Brent Schweitzer, threw herself into her work to nurse her broken heart. The effect was less than impressive in terms of mending her heart. However, the work Anna produced was extremely impressive. A little of the groundwork had already been laid in the field she chose: string theory, specifically elasticity in string dynamics. But, it was Anna's wholehearted, brokenhearted work that pushed the field to the point of usefulness (a point that much physics never reaches). Work was started on designing the first elasti-drive spaceship. At this point, Brent was still only twenty-three years old.

By the time the ship was designed, built, named the *Peter Rabbit* (the Principal Elite given the honor of naming it had a three-year-old daughter and a fondness for ancient, pre-Expansionism literature), and sitting on Wespirtech's airfield, Brent Schweitzer was in his late thirties. Building the second ship, appropriately named the *Mr. McGregor*, would have been a lot faster, if Brent hadn't stolen all the design plans and records along with the prototype ship... and if Anna had still been mending her broken heart. Unfortunately for the program, Anna's productivity had been severely cut down by her meeting a nice chemist, who was better at returning her affections.

Thus, although the police program had moved with as much haste as possible, Officers Cicero and Hyland were still thirty years behind their culprit simply because it took that long to build another ship capable of comparable speeds. With thirty years and all the technology he'd stolen, there was no telling what Brent Schweitzer could have accomplished, or consequently of what the officers would face. Cicero was very excited. Hyland was nervous. Neither of them, after the long months hopping from star to star, checking all the likely, habitable planets for signs of the *Peter Rabbit*, felt terribly ready for this moment, so close to what they'd sought for so long.

Cicero and Hyland disembarked the *Mr. McGregor*, holding standard issue, police elasti-blasters in their hands. They looked around, cautiously. It was a beautiful world. Neither of them had been to planet Da Vinci, both having been born on poorer, less scenic worlds, or they would have noticed the similarity. As it was, Cicero from the dusty, red world of Glencora, and Hyland from a small, colony on Isleydora's sterile moon were both awed.

The sky of Schweitzer's chosen planet was a blue so deep that, like a sun-kissed ocean, it hinted at green. The trees in the distance swayed, bending in the breeze, and Cicero suspected he could hear music carried in the air, emanating from the breeze drawn bends and fluttering leaves of those distant trees. Perhaps more impressive than the hint of music, or at least more noticeable to Hyland's less discerning senses, were the colors flushed through the trees' leaves. One moment, the whole forest was green like any other, then at the behest of some unknown source, crimsons and scarlets chased each other from tree to tree, as if the trees were blushing. A moment later, the same repeated but with purples, yellows, or blues. It was inspiring, and it was clearly Brent's work.

Walking across the grassy ground from the *Mr. McGregor* to the *Peter Rabbit*, Cicero noted that the grass blushed around his feet, similarly to the way colors chased each other across the trees. Cicero was very excited. Reaching the *Peter Rabbit's* main hatch, Cicero and Hyland took flanking positions on either side of the door. Then, Cicero reached out and pounded twice on the door. He called out, "Schweitzer? Are you inside?" He expected to wait and receive no response. Why would Schweitzer be waiting for them? Nonetheless, and to Cicero's great surprise, although the hatch didn't swing open, a voice called out: "I'm around back!"

Cicero and Hyland looked at each other, their faces mirrors of each other in surprise. Eventually, regaining his composure, Cicero shrugged, and started heading around back, blaster still in hand. Hyland followed. The sight that greeted their eyes, as they rounded the bend and arrived behind the ship, was a man lying on the grass in the shade, hands folded behind his head. "Hi," the man said as he heard them approach. "Welcome to my planet."

Cicero took a moment to size up the man: trimly built, approximately six feet tall, clean shaven, and his head topped with white hair. The man was believably Brent Schweitzer, and, furthermore, his face matched the picture on the cover of Gloria van Santen's biography... oh, and the pictures in the police report as well. Cicero remained professionally calm. "Brent Schweitzer," he said, "we're here to arrest you on charges of grand theft and treason."

"Hmm," Brent observed. "You know, I rather expected you to land in that field over there... " he gestured ahead of him. Then, looking up and noticing the elasti-blasters in Cicero and Hyland's hands, he added, "I've never seen those before. I wonder if they're Anna's work. May I look at one?"

"Of course you may not!" Hyland blurted out, surprised and bemused by a prisoner *asking* his apprehenders to simply turn over their weapons. Then Hyland's surprise was pushed to shock as his commanding officer, who should have known better despite his preoccupations and general foolishness, did flip the blaster around in his hand and merely render it to their culprit. Hyland was annoyed.

"They stem from the same principle as the elasti-drive," Cicero said to Brent, ignoring his inferior officer's outburst. "We call them elasti-blasters. I think they're pretty much the next thing Ms. Karlingoff worked on after you left."

Brent looked the blaster over and handed it back. "I'm glad to see she kept getting such good work done, but how do you come to know so much about it? Last I knew, the general public wasn't much interested in keeping up on who invented their technological progress for them."

"Officer Cicero here is your biggest fan," Hyland said dryly. "Can we get on with this?"

Spurred by Hyland's reminder, Cicero informed Brent that he would show them the ship and all the technology he had stolen, so they could take inventory. All of it would have to be returned, or else it would add to the charges hanging over Brent's head. Brent complied, and every piece of technology was still intact, in working order, and already loaded onto the *Peter Rabbit*.

"I anticipated your coming," Schweitzer explained. "I knew someone would come after me someday, so when I finished my original work here, I put all the machinery back. Once I had my world running, I didn't need it anymore."

An uncomfortable silence filled the well-packed ship as Brent and Cicero both struggled against asking the questions they wanted to ask, hoping the other would ask first. Schweitzer wanted to ask if they'd like to see his world, and Cicero wanted to ask if he'd be willing to show it. Hyland just wanted the tension to break, so he asked Brent in Cicero's stead, "Would you like to show us around, and get a last look yourself, before we have to take you home?" Brent replied that he'd be pleased to.

~

WHEN BRENT FIRST landed the *Peter Rabbit* on his new world, it was already a beautiful one. Brent chose it, during his long years of silent planning at Wespirtech, because of its likely similarities to Da Vinci. On his arrival, he was not disappointed. A temperate, virgin planet awaited his artistic, scientific touch. After thirty long years, the young planet had evolved and matured, under Brent's directing hand, into the fantastical menagerie which greeted his police officer guests' eyes. Cicero was delighted, and Hyland was awed in spite of himself.

The first creature the three of them met, on their walk through Schweitzer's fairy land, was a glittering, golden butterfly. Brent hadn't changed it much from its original genetic design, but as it flitted closer, Cicero could just make out what looked like writing on its wings. Schweitzer smiled, and explained that the writing was poetry. He'd written the poetry into their genes, and all the butterflies emerged from their chrysalises with snatches of the psalms emblazoned on the glory of their wings.

Hyland watched the butterfly glide away, towards the edge of the rainbowing forest, and was struck to the heart when he saw the butterfly land. As a child, Hyland had cherished a secret love for unicorns, that had gotten him teased when discovered more than once. The butterfly landed on a shining, white, perfectly real and corporeal unicorn's horn.

From cloven hoof to clockwise twisting horn, the unicorn was exactly as Hyland had imagined them. The eyes were deep and enigmatic, too deep to clearly be a specific color. The face was thin and framed by the curly locks of a flowing mane. The tail was long and tufted at the end like a lion's. And every inch of the unicorn, except for its piercing, dark eyes, was the softest white.

When Cicero saw the charmingly mythical beast, he laughed outright from joy. Perhaps on another world, in another mood, the creature might have looked merely silly, but here, in such a forest, it looked beautiful and perfectly in place.

"I made them from a combination of deer and mountain goat genes," Schweitzer said. "And the horn is like the horn on ancient Earth's narwhales."

Even knowing the unicorns' genetic sources couldn't break the tiny, elegant beast's spell. Cicero and Hyland watched raptly, dumbstruck, until the unicorn grew tired of watching them back, turned tail, and sallied away between the trees.

Brent watched his guests' faces, enjoying their reactions. After giving them a moment to recover from the mystical vision of a real, live unicorn, Brent led them after it into the trees. Walking among the trees, the faint music Cicero had earlier perceived grew clearer, emanating, in stereo, all around them. The music of the trees, for it plainly came from them, sounded much like the discordant, yet oddly pleasant sound of an all strings orchestra tuning up, or of a choir preparing to sing, each choral member warming up his voice separately. The effect was soothing and naturally unobtrusive like the sound of a distant waterfall.

Brent and his guests emerged from the forest on the edge of a small village. Columns of smoke rose from the chimneys of small, hut-like buildings with thatched roofs. Villagers busied themselves among the buildings. A woman tended a central fire; a man sat, leaning against a building, shucking husks from an unusual looking, blue fruit; a few children chased after each other, ducking behind buildings, in and out of each others' sight.

Coming from their months on a gleamingly new space ship and their years in the technologically advanced and overly machined society of the Human Expansion, Cicero and Hyland might have been tempted to view the scene before them as squalid, a horrifying way to live. Yet... the villagers all looked so happy... and they were all so strangely beautiful...

The woman, kneeling before the fire, particularly caught Cicero's eye. Her hair was long and fell like a cascade of glass over her shoulders, framing her triangular face. It was so fine and blonde, so blonde as to almost look clear. Her ears, peaking from behind her nearly fiber-optic hair, were gracefully pointed, as any elf's should be, for elves were clearly what Schweitzer had created here. The woman, like all her fellow elfin-folk, was small, her total height bringing her still short of the policemen's shoulders.

As the three men walked by, the elfin-woman rose and looked at Brent questioningly. "Not now, Kylani," he said. "I have visitors. They and I must talk."

"Brandon's out checking on the carnivorous plants," the woman said, in a tonal voice, "so your hut is empty."

"Thank you," Brent replied, "we'll be there."

By the time the three men found themselves safely inside, door closed behind them, Cicero was nearly bursting with questions. Yet, in Cicero's indecision as to which question to ask first, Hyland was the first to speak. "You chose an inhabited planet? What have you done? Set yourself up as God here? Preying on an innocent, pre-technological race?"

Brent looked surprised for a moment, then said, "No, no, you don't understand. I created them, but they don't think of me as a god... merely an elderly, sometimes forgetful story-teller... perhaps something of a grandfather. I seem ancient to them."

Hyland looked at a loss, and Cicero seemed only moderately more illuminated.

"You know the inventory of technology I brought," Brent continued. "It was more than sufficient to create the first of them... they were only babies, and I had to raise them myself, but they grow up fast. They only live about twenty years."

Hyland looked surprised. "You were working on extending life... " he said.

The following silence was extremely uncomfortable as each of the three men pursued their own and very different thoughts. Brent was reminded of the plague he'd pushed far from his mind: the years of studying life extension, trapped in the steel box known as Wespirtech, on a barren moon. Twenty years, he thought, was plenty for a happy life time... he'd lived more than twenty good years, between those of his childhood and the thirty years spent here. But he would have traded the extra ones to not be faced by the years he imagined stretching out before him. He would have been happy to die there on his own world, surrounded by his people, his children.

Hyland was too young to understand Brent's thoughts. He tried, but couldn't fathom why a man with immortality almost in his grasp, for such had been the promise of Brent's research, would willingly choose a life surrounded by death... and, worse, the deaths, the frequent deaths, of such beautiful creatures. Hyland wished he could return home, bringing not just the infamous Brent Schweitzer, but also bringing the end to the end of life as well. What a waste Brent Schweitzer had made of his life, a life that held such promise. Perhaps, returned to the society of the Human Expansion, and faced with the choice of ending his life in prison or returning to his work, Schweitzer would make the right choice.

This time, Cicero was the first to speak: "Can we meet them, talk to your people?" he asked.

"Certainly," Brent said, heavy with the weight of time. "You can stay and explore while I go find my son. I'll want to say goodbye to Brandon before you take me away."

BRENT SET OFF towards the grove of carnivorous plants, where his son Brandon was last seen headed, with a heavy heart. Hyland and Cicero stayed behind with lighter, yet still troubled, feelings. Hyland stood stiffly by as Cicero approached and began talking to Kylani. She was, at first, reluctant, due possibly to being shy, but eventually her curiosity warmed her demeanor. After asking about Cicero and Hyland's uniforms, blasters, ship, and lives back home, she suddenly looked pensive. Her brow furrowed, and she bit her lip. "What will happen to Brent when you take him back?" she asked. "He said you'd probably take him away... but he never told any of us what you'll do with him."

Cicero smiled warmly. "You have no need to worry," he said. "He'll be well taken care of. He's already turned over everything he'd stolen, so the courts will go easy on him. Probably, he'll just return to the work he was doing before he came here."

"What did he do?" Kylani asked, with a simplicity that was disconcerting. Had he really never told them?

Hyland stepped forward to answer *this* question. "Brent Schweitzer was trying to discover a way to extend human life. It was a noble cause."

Kylani looked surprised. "But, Brent's already lived so long," she said. "Brent was there when my mother was born. He outlived her, and he says he'll outlive me, as well as my son. Why would he want to live any longer?"

"Wouldn't you like to live longer?" Hyland asked, feeling a spark of outrage, deep down, at what Schweitzer had done in creating such a short-lived race.

Kylani frowned. "I'm afraid of dying, if that's what you mean. But... is running away from it the answer?"

"What about your son?" Hyland pressed, beginning to express his outrage in his voice. "What about when he dies?"

Kylani looked at a loss. "Leave her alone," Cicero said. Then, more gently, he added "I think my subordinate and I need to talk alone. I'm sorry if we've upset you." Then, turning to Hyland and roughly grabbing him at the elbow, Cicero withdrew. The two officers removed themselves from the village, as far as the edge of the forest. Hyland leaned, nonchalantly, against one of the trees. It's leaves fluttered and sang in objection, but Hyland didn't mind.

"What were you trying to do?" Cicero asked, looking back towards the village. "Did you just want to upset her?"

Hyland looked down at the ground and scuffed his feet, kicking an unusually star-like pinecone. "I don't like what he's done to them. He should have used his brilliance to save lives, not end them."

"Schweitzer isn't the one that kills them."

"I know," Hyland said. "But he made them that way. He made them to die."

"They die because they live, and they only live because Schweitzer bothered to make them at all."

Hyland and Cicero stared at each other levelly for a few minutes. "You're such a fan," Hyland muttered to himself to break the tension. Then each of them turned to watch the village. Kylani was still at the fire, but a young boy, who must have been the son she mentioned, had joined her. He was smiling and clapping his hands.

"They seem happy," Cicero said. "That's all anyone can ask out of life. Some people live scores of years without ever being as happy as the people look here."

Hyland looked around with the corner of his eye, as if saying he wanted to be convinced. He wanted his mind to be made easier.

"We didn't come here on a quest after some magic elixir," Cicero said. "We came because we're police officers, and a man stole a spaceship and a lot of expensive equipment. That man happens to be brilliant... he may even hold the secret to human immortality... but getting it out of him is not our job. Our job is to bring back what was stolen."

Hyland nodded. "I had hopes... " he said.

"I know you did."

The next few minutes passed in silence, but it was a much easier silence than the last. Cicero and Hyland watched Kylani playing a game with her son, in front of the fire. When Brent returned, he was with another, younger man, who looked just like Brent had back when he'd been researching at Wespirtech. The younger man was clearly Brandon, the son after whom Brent went looking. Cicero theorized that rather than a normal son, Brandon was probably an exact clone, raised as a son.

The older and younger Schweitzer joined Kylani at the fire. As they talked to her, others of the elfin-folk began to gather. There were hugs, warm handshakes, and sad smiles passed around. Brent was saying his goodbyes. Kylani's son, before so happy, now broke into tears, and she tried to cheer him. Finally, Brent gave a long hug to his own son and went back into his hut, apparently to gather his things to leave.

Cicero, still at the edge of the forest, was deeply moved by this display. He turned urgently to Hyland, and said "I want to let him go. I want to let him stay here."

"Let him go... " Hyland repeated with astonishment. "You were just talking about our job... "

"We'd bring the ship and the machinery back... everything he stole. We'd just leave him."

Hyland continued to look surprised, and Cicero was clearly agitated.

"We'd say we couldn't find him," Cicero said, "... that he must have left the ship, that he must have died." Cicero looked earnestly at Hyland. "I want to do this, because I think it's the right thing to do."

Hyland, still recovering from his hopes of returning with an elixir of life, or at least a scientist likely to create one, looked skeptical. "He's a criminal," Hyland said.

"He's a thief," Cicero agreed. "He set back the Human Expansion's space program at Wespirtech by a solid twenty years... but he belongs here. I know why he left now... and I don't want to be the one to take him back."

Hyland perked up for a moment. "You know why he left? Why did he leave?"

"Have you ever talked to a Keat?" Cicero asked.

"What's that got to do with anything?"

"Have you?"

"No, I haven't."

"They're quite amazing conversationalists," Cicero said. "I talked to one once. I was waiting in line for a spaceflight home. There was an Anathoran diplomat waiting too. I'd have talked to him with the Keat translating, but he'd fallen asleep. The Keat talked to me anyway... " Cicero looked ponderous, like his thoughts were a hundred million miles and twenty years away.

"And so?" Hyland prompted.

"The point," Cicero concluded once recalled to his senses, "is that no one knows how interesting the Keats are... no one ever talks to them. We just use them. If I were Schweitzer, I wouldn't be happy with that. To create such beautiful things and to see them go unappreciated... "

Hyland frowned. "You're quite a romantic for a police officer," he said.

Cicero chuckled at that. "Schweitzer's quite a romantic for a scientist," he said. Then, returning to his point: "I want to do this, but I can't do it without you."

"I don't know... " Hyland muttered without promise.

"If you won't go along with it... " Cicero began, but didn't finish, knowing that Hyland knew full well his power to deny Cicero's treasonous plan. Furthermore, it was at this point that Brent emerged from his hut, a small bag slung over his shoulder. Thus, Cicero and Hyland's argument, already dying, was put to a complete stop by Brent and Brandon joining them.

Brent smiled weakly to the policemen and introduced his son. "This is Brandon," he said, as Brandon reached out and shook each of the officer's hands. "I cloned myself twenty years ago to create him," Brent explained, looking proudly at his son. "I made him so that he could stay here and take care of my world when you came... I knew you'd come... " Brent trailed off, losing his composure. "I'm ready," he said. Then, looking a last time at his son, Brent said, with passion tingeing his voice, "Take care of my world, Brandon... and *enjoy* it."

Brandon made an almost entirely successful effort not to look like a child who'd been given clothes for Christmas, leading Cicero to suspect Brandon was less thrilled with his father's world than Brent himself was. He smiled, patted Brent on the back, and said "Take care, Dad."

Cicero gave a last, imploring look to Hyland, before giving up his hopes. Cicero, Schweitzer, and Hyland turned to leave, two of them more reluctantly than the third. After the first few steps, their departure was interrupted by an unhappy cry from behind. Hyland turned around to see Kylani's son, having run after them, wrapped, clinging, around Schweitzer leg. Kylani stood a few paces behind, looking embarrassed. "I'm sorry... " she said. "I tried to catch him... He says he won't let you leave... " The boy's elfin face was buried in the crook of Schweitzer's knee.

Brent prepared to speak, but Hyland's conscience could support him no more. "You can stay," he said. "We'll let you stay."

Years of weight dropped from Brent's shoulders, and Cicero smacked Hyland heartily on the back. "I *knew* you'd come around," he said.

"Come around?" Hyland said, returning to his usual

dryness. "I don't know what you're talking about. This man couldn't possibly be Brent Schweitzer."

"That's the spirit," Cicero said, and then, turning to Brent, Brandon, Kylani, and the small boy, Cicero explained the plan. As soon as the idea sunk into Kylani's boy's head, a broad grin broke across his face. Hyland had never felt more like a hero than at that moment.

Cicero and Hyland walked back to the *Peter Rabbit* and *Mr. McGregor*, thinking about the wonders they'd seen and feeling good about the choices they'd made. As the two of them stood, between the ships, arguing over who would get to try flying the *Peter Rabbit,* and who had to go back to the *Mr. McGregor*, Brandon came running up. Breathless, Brandon stopped before them. "I want to come," he said in huffs, while regaining his breath. "I want to come."

Cicero and Hyland exchanged a glance, but before either of them could speak, Brandon continued. "I've never seen another world. I know it's beautiful here. I love it here. But, I want to see what else is out there... this is all my father wants, but... "

"But you're not him," Hyland finished for him.

"We've already said our goodbyes," Brandon said. "I can leave immediately. Can you smuggle me back? Will it raise too many questions? I could say I saw my father die... "

"We'll figure it out," Cicero said. "For now, the question is whether you want to ride with me on the *Peter Rabbit*, or go with Hyland on the *Mr. McGregor*... "

Hyland glared his objection at Cicero, and the ensuing argument took some time, but ended satisfactorily for Hyland. He got to fly the *Peter Rabbit*. Brandon stowed away with him, planning to hide among the many extra pieces of technology when they returned, so that he could slip away while it was being inventoried. Slip away and find his way among the many, confusing worlds of the Human Expansion...

The ships took off from Schweitzer's idyllic little world, powered their elasti-drives, and barreled their way home. Even the sun that warmed Schweitzer and his village receded into the distance. Brandon was excited, but he realized that he would sincerely miss his father and his home. And, yet, there was no telling what he could create when he joined the scientists of the Human Expansion.

LUNAR CAVITY

The air was too cold and the gravity too strong. But, Druthel liked the cave-like architecture. He was on the moon-world of Kong-Fuzi, a naked rock without even an atmosphere—only a few small atmo-domes, a scattering of boxy, airtight buildings, and a subterranean tunnel complex connecting them all. It circled the planet Da Vinci, capital of the Human Expansion, and it hosted the renowned and arrogantly named Wespirtech, the Western Spiral Arm Institute of Technology.

As if humans were the only species with a science institute in the western spiral arm of the galaxy...

Druthel stretched his long arms, unfurling their expanses of leathery wing-skin, and refolded them about his narrow body in the other order. He lost some of the warmth that his winged arms had been holding in, but the bite of the chilled air against the thin fur on his outer arm had simply become too much.

"Are you uncomfortable?" the small human administrator asked. It wasn't the first time he'd shown concern for Druthel's physical comfort, but there was nothing he could do about the gravity. And there was nothing he chose to do about the temperature.

"I'll be fine," Druthel said, quietly in his own language. A translator clipped to his inadequately warm waistcoat repeated his words in the Solanese that the human would understand. "My home world, however..."

"Right," the human said, bristling. "We've been working as quickly as we can. This all would have gone much faster if your planet had established terms for scientific trades with the Expansion before... well..."

Before we needed to, Druthel thought.

"Nonetheless, my superiors seem to think we can accept the contract in the form we hammered out yesterday," the human said. "As a preliminary contract anyway."

The human's strange Solanese words, a bizarre, continuous, monotone in Druthel's tufted black ears, came to life for him as he heard them repeated by the translator. The human smiled thinly as he waited for Druthel's response. He was expecting a thank you, perhaps. Instead, Druthel said simply, "Then we can begin?"

"As soon as the team's ready," the human said.

Druthel twitched the leathery nose at the end of his long, brown-furred muzzle. "I will go prepare the ship." The translator at his waistcoat was still droning away in Solanese as Druthel shuffled, awkwardly in the heavy gravity, out of the administrator's office. He wandered down the tunnel-like hallway of that foreign moon towards the starship bay where his vessel waited to take him and the team of human scientists he'd come to fetch back to Wrombarra. When the humans were ready, he would fly them triumphantly from this moon to the empty lunar cavity, many light-years away, where the moon that once orbited his homeworld used to be.

Thinking of the task that awaited them there, Druthel's arms loosed around his cold body, and his wings began to drag.

THE HUMAN SCIENTISTS with their flat-yet-knobbly pink faces appeared one-by-one in the open door of the airlock to Druthel's spaceship. He watched each of them spring up the steps from the airlock to the ship's antechamber as if the gravity here was nothing to them—which, of course, it was. Gravity isn't especially noticeable until it's wrong.

He checked each scientist off in his mind as they arrived. He'd been thoroughly briefed on the scientists he was being sent to fetch. In fact, he'd been intimately involved in picking them. From the holos included in the bios on their various academic publications, he was able to recognize them each on sight: Jon Einray, the hulking male chrono-physicist; Anna Karlingoff, the dun-haired female string-theorist who had invented the elasti-drive; Ivan Bower, the male chemist clinging possessively to Anna's hand; the four male geologists whose addition to the team depressed Druthel to no end; and, finally...

There was one scientist missing.

Druthel followed the group of humans inside to where they were settling into hammocks slung about the spaceship's central lounge, stowing their bags into netting around the edges of the room. "Excuse me," Druthel said. "One of you is missing. The one called..." He tried to annunciate the strange Solanese name, but his mouth and tongue simply weren't formed for it.

The human called Ivan spoke, and a moment later the translator told Druthel, "Rhiannon? She says she's not coming. We should go without her."

"That is not acceptable." Druthel shuffled his arms, flapping the expanse of wing stretched between them and his narrow body. The human named Rhiannon was a quantum chemist, one of the least distinguished scientists he'd been sent to fetch, but the one whose previous work had the most bearing on the problem at hand. "One of you will take me to her, yes?" he said.

Ivan shrugged, but Anna nodded. "Sure," she said. Then, turning to the chemist who was clearly her mate, "Ivan, go show Druthel the way to Rhiannon's room."

Druthel was inexperienced with human facial expressions, but Ivan seemed less than pleased. The edges of his mouth turned downward as Ivan unwrapped his arms from Anna's shoulders. "Yeah, sure, it's this way," he said, climbing out of the hammock and heading for the ship's airlock. Druthel followed him off the ship, through the docking bay, and into the corridors of Kong-Fuzi.

Druthel lost his breath, trying to keep up with the bounding Ivan. He leaned against the hallway walls with unfurled wings, but Ivan only slowed down at the ends of corridors, looking back to make sure Druthel didn't completely lose his way.

"This one," Ivan said, knocking on a slate gray door that sported a scribble-screen on it, covered in colorful, indecipherable Solanese writing. "Hey Rhiannon!" Ivan called through the closed door, "The wrombarr wants to see you!" To Druthel, he said, "The rest's up to you." Ivan disappeared back down the hall at the same time as the door to Rhiannon's room slid open.

THE YOUNG WOMAN sitting on the bed was clearly sad. Her wilted posture transcended culture. "You can come in," she said to the furry-winged alien standing in the door. She heard her voice translated into a series of high pitched chirps and squeals by a device clipped to his clothing. "Sit down," she said, gesturing to the empty bed across the room from her—another single-size bunk, but this one unclothed with sheets or blankets.

Druthel shuffled in and contrived to fold his body up onto the strangely flat, horizontal surface. His long, slender limbs angled awkwardly inside the flaps of his wings, but he managed a passable approximation of the way that the human Rhiannon sat on the mirroring bunk.

She was small. Smaller than the other human scientists, and the long fur that crowned her head was thicker, frizzier. It fell to her shoulders, framing her pale, naked face and completely covering her ears. Druthel's own ears flicked on the top of his head, reflecting his thoughts as he wondered at what emotions those buried ears might hide.

"You are not ready?" Druthel asked. Her side of the room was filled with alien looking belongings. But there was nothing that resembled the packed bags that the other scientists had carried onto his ship. "I can help you pack, yes?"

The slight pink of the lips on Rhiannon's strangely flat muzzle thinned. "I'm not coming," she said. "I'm sorry. I thought the others would tell you that."

"They did," Druthel said. "But that is not acceptable."

His own lips, along his narrow muzzle tightened as well. For the first time, he felt the layer of fur that covered his face as a kind of shield, hiding the vulnerable expression of emotions beneath. In contrast, flickers of expression danced across the vulnerably bare skin of Rhiannon's face. Her delicate lips turned down; the skin between her eyes tightened into creases. But for only a moment.

"There's nothing you need from me," she said, "that Anna, Jon, Ivan, and the others can't provide."

"That's not true—" Druthel began, but Rhiannon continued to speak, the translator chirping away after her.

"I've read the abstract you submitted describing..." she said.

"And I've read all your papers," Druthel said, not waiting for either Rhiannon or the translator to finish speaking. "They are brilliant..."

"... the terrible predicament that your world is in..."

One wromabarr, one human, and two electronic voices from the translator continued to speak until the word "predicament" reached Druthel's tall, pointed ears.

"Predicament!" he exclaimed, slicing Rhiannon's voice to a halt, although the translator continued to chirp and drone away. "You call it only a predicament?"

She must have heard the distress and despair in his tone, despite the alien nature of his voice. "I'm sorry," she said. "I didn't mean to..."

"Our moon is gone," Druthel said. "The hole it left behind —" His chirpy voice choked away, as he thought of all his friends and family back on Wrombarra. He quickly composed himself. He had a task to do. He must right what had gone wrong. To do that, he needed Rhiannon. "Do you know what kind of effects it has on a planet to suddenly remove such a massive source of gravitational pull?" he asked her.

Rhiannon lowered her dark eyes.

"Earthquakes, tsunamis, volcanoes... massive geological instability." The words were hard to say. He felt that each time he named one of these horrible side-effects that he might be conjuring one to crush loved ones, light years away, back on Wrombarra. "And that is only the beginning..."

In the silence after his voice trailed off, Rhiannon whispered, "I know." Her eyes were still downcast. "But, I'm not a geologist. I can't help with any of that."

"Geologists won't fix this!" Druthel exclaimed.

"The geologists can suggest ways to counteract the seismic shifting..."

"Bandages," Druthel said, ignoring Rhiannon's and the translator's words. "We need a cure not a bandage. We need our moon back or, over time, our whole world will die."

Rhiannon didn't tell Druthel what a long shot that was, pulling their moon back from the depths of hyperspace. They both knew he was hoping for a miracle. A miracle to counteract a catastrophe. But, then, the Wromabarran Empire, a single planet's worth of reclusive winged sapients, wouldn't have given up their pride and come asking for help if they weren't at the very end of their options. Druthel had been sent to the Human Expansion; another ambassador was sent to the Lintar Oligarchy; a third had been sent to wrangle any possible help from the diffuse and disorganized Srellick Mercenary Syndicate.

Of those options, Druthel truly felt that the small female primate in front of him was his people's best hope.

The reptilian srellick were brilliant, but it was unlikely that their most relevant scientists could be located in time. The methane-breathing lintar were simply too alien. Druthel didn't think that their scientists and his own could learn to work together... perhaps ever. And that's assuming they'd deign to come. Nonetheless, his people were losing their independence, merely to ask for the unlikely chance of help.

"My planet needs you," Druthel said.

Rhiannon wrapped her stick-like arms, bare of the expanse of wing-skin on a wrombarran, about her body. Her shoulders lifted and dropped. Her down-turned mouth, her downcast eyes... everything about her bespoke depression.

More importantly, Druthel realized, his pleas weren't working. "Fine," Druthel said. He would change tactics. It would help if he knew what was upsetting this human... There were so many possibilities, and he wasn't even an expert at understanding the emotions of his own race. Let alone the emotions of an alien. "You do not wish to help an alien race," he said, testing for her reaction.

At that, her eyes flashed up. She stared at him for a long moment before speaking. "Your people have their own scientists." The words were slow, measured. "You're a scientist."

Druthel averred.

"Then you fix it," Rhiannon said.

Druthel didn't know if her tone was harsh, but her words certainly were. "I am doing everything I know how," Druthel said, fighting the pain and anger. "If I can fix this, believe me, I will." His tall ears were flat against his head, but his eyes held steady on her alien face. "Right now, Rhiannon, that means convincing you to come to Wrombarra."

Rhiannon twisted her short, webless fingers together. "Scientists trifling with science got you into this," she said. "What makes you think one more scientist will help?"

Druthel's ears straightened. He rearranged his long arms on the uncomfortably flat surface. With nothing for his fingertips to cling to, the expanses of his wings were forced to rest, distorted on the mattress. He wanted this conversation to be over. He wanted Rhiannon to be safely ensconced in a hammock on his ship, so he could take her back to Wrombarra, where he could show her the records of his work—his fateful work—and pick her brain for ideas at leisure. Well, as much leisure as the death throes of his world would afford them.

"What else," Druthel said, "do you suggest? I came all this way, at a time when my world needs me more than ever, to hear your suggestions. So, please, tell me. If you have a better idea than pleading for help from the Wespirtech expert on hyperspatial quantum chemistry, then I would be honored to hear it." The sarcastic ring to his voice would not translate, but Druthel hoped she'd infer it. Assuming these humans understood sarcasm.

Rhiannon's mouth opened as if to speak, but she hesitated instead. Then, too quietly for the translator to pick up, she mouthed the words, "Quit trifling with science. But, then, that's not really an option for you now. Besides, it's really advice for me." When she raised her voice, she simply said, "I'll come."

Though, she thought, this may be the last work of science I commit.

BACK ON THE SHIP, Druthel made sure the humans were all settled in their hammocks before take-off. The sensation of gravity rose and then fell as Druthel piloted the ship up to the proper speed for threading its way into the shallowest layer of hyperspace, barely skimming the surface of that parallel dimension. He set the controls on auto-pilot, and then he went back to join the humans.

The hyperspace trip would take three days, and he hoped to learn a little about the different personalities of the human scientists in that time. Ideally, he would have liked to begin working with them, but, realistically, they'd need at least that much time to catch up on the records of the state of wrombarran research concerning their missing moon stored in the ship's computer banks.

Druthel helped the humans out of their hammocks, and he showed them how to work the computers. All the records had already been translated into Solanese, albeit quickly and shoddily. There wasn't time for anything better. So, for a start, that would have to do. Druthel could help them when they got stuck.

"Well, look at—"

"Will you...—...?"

"Wouldn't you..."

"Huh, that's really—"

Druthel's ears skewed. One flattened against his head, and the other, he forced to stand tall. He tried to listen to the human scientists. He really did. But, his little electronic translator simply couldn't keep up with so many different voices talking at once.

The longer Druthel listened, the more he began to panic. He could tell that the geologists were excited about something, and the scientist named Einray seemed from his posture to be in a deep debate with Ivan... But, Druthel simply couldn't make out their words. This would be a big problem, presenting an insufferable bottleneck to communication when they were all back on Wrombarra. There would be twice as many scientists speaking at once there—all these humans, and even more wrombarrans. Hopefully a few srellick or lintar...

It would not be good. They would all have to take turns, speaking slowly, and it would take forever to get anything done.

Deeply troubled, Druthel left the humans to their incomprehensible confusion of work and headed to the helm. He couldn't help them directly, but, he could try to make them more comfortable. The human scientists looked awkward in zero gee. They had trouble grappling with the wrombarran hammocks, and their wingless arms gave them little traction against the atmosphere.

After his stay at Wespirtech, Druthel sympathized, but he didn't have artificial gravity to offer them on this ship. So, he turned the temperature down lower than he'd have liked in deference to what he knew of their preferred climate. He adjusted their course, and then set the controls back on autopilot.

He knew he couldn't understand what the humans were saying, but, maybe he could learn more about their personalities by observing them. He was about to go back to the hold to check on the humans when three brightly colored avians, each about the size of his head, came flapping into the helm of the ship.

"No pets!" Druthel exclaimed. "No pets!" He realized immediately where they'd come from: one of the geologists, along with his backpack of personal affects, had brought a large, gilded cage when he boarded the ship. Druthel would have objected when he first saw it, but the cage had been covered with a cloth. And Druthel lacked the cultural knowledge necessary to realize what was inside.

Of course, the ship was already threading through hyperspace now, so it was too late to take the birds back. They would have to stay, but Druthel planned to tell the humans they had to keep the birds in their cage.

Before Druthel made a move, however, the first of the three birds, perching with its claws clasping the netting of Druthel's hammock said, "We're not pets." The bird, with its brilliant red-and-green plumage, spoke in Solanese, but Druthel's electronic translator repeated the words in Wrimbrin.

The second bird—this one had flat gray colored feathers—said, "We're here to learn your language."

"We're called Keats," said the third bird, a blue-and-gold creature. "We're genetically engineered for facility with languages. If you'll talk to us in yours, then we can learn it before we reach Wrombarra."

Druthel looked at the little animals. They were, in a strange way, less alien than the humans. Despite their diminutive sizes, the Keats' winged bodies made them more similar to wrombarrans. "Can you really do that?" Druthel asked, barely daring to hope. He didn't see how a pet bird could do better than his electronic translator, but, if there was even a chance...

All three birds bobbed their heads enthusiastically in the gesture humans used for 'yes.' "Oh, definitely!" the blue-and-gold bird said.

"All right," Druthel said. It was certainly worth a try. "What am I supposed to talk about?"

The red-and-green bird cocked its head, listening to both Druthel's words and the translation. "Anything!" it said.

"Everything!" the blue-and-gold bird added.

The gray bird introduced the three of them as Coco, Lulu, and Joni, gesturing with her beak toward the red-and-green bird, the blue-and-gold bird, and herself, respectively.

❦

TRUE TO THEIR WORD, the three Keats listened faithfully to anything and everything Druthel felt like telling them, and they quickly began to pick up his language. To begin with, Druthel tried to tell the Keats useful stories about the history of his world, but, before long, he found himself rambling to them about his own life.

While he was talking to the Keats, though, Druthel was watching Rhiannon. Her thick, dark mane shielded her pale face from him. She didn't look at him. But, then, she didn't look at the other humans either.

Druthel knew only the smallest fragments of Solanese himself, so he couldn't catch any of the meaning in her infrequent conversations with the other scientists. But, he could see the patterns in her body language.

She sat apart from the others. She spoke less. Her shoulders stayed hunched; her limbs held close. She was a being turned inward, and Druthel found the mystery of what was happening inside that withdrawn, alien mind enthralling.

When they arrived at Wrombarra, Druthel's living cargo—Keat and human—would be swept away in a storm of other wrombarran scientists. Ideally, the humans' addition to the storm would spark lightening flashes of brilliance that could be used to save his planet by recalling their lost moon from the depths of hyperspace. But, Druthel was worried that Rhiannon, who he felt could be instrumental at the center of that storm, would instead keep to herself.

"Do you know the scientists you work with well?" Druthel asked the Keats on the last day of their flight. If he could only figure out what troubled her, maybe he could incite her to participate in the coming storm of scientific creative energy.

"I've worked with Karlingoff!" Joni answered. She'd learned enough of Druthel's language already, the dominant language on Wrombarra to answer without the help of his electronic translator.

The other two Keats demurred. "We're younger," Coco explained, arching her red-and-green wings. "Lulu and I, this is our first mission."

"Though, none of us Keats have worked much with some of them," Joni said. "Einray, for instance, almost never leaves Wespirtech."

"What about Rhiannon?" Druthel asked, pressing for more information.

Joni turned to the other Keats. They conferred quickly in a language that didn't sound like Solanese to Druthel, and his electronic translator certainly had no luck with it. He'd heard the Keats use it with each other during the last few days, and, his best guess was that it was some sort of pidgin, combining pieces of the massive number of languages each of the Keats knew. They were proficient not only in Solanese and now, largely, in Wrimbrin, but also in dozens more languages used by species scattered throughout the galaxy and many sub-cultures of the Human Expansion itself.

"Rhiannon is usually reclusive like Einray," Coco said, switching back to Wrimbrin. "But, recently, she's been working a lot with a biologist—"

"Her roommate," Lulu interjected.

"—and their project involved more travel and networking," Coco said, without acknowledging the interruption from her blue-and-gold compatriot.

"None of us three worked with them, though," Joni said.

Druthel thought about the empty half of Rhiannon's room back at Wespirtech. "Did her roommate leave?" he asked.

"Leave? Leave where?" Coco said.

"She's a biologist," Lulu said. "She didn't leave with us, because she couldn't help with your moon."

"Unless it's not really a moon!" Coco said. "Maybe it's a giant space animal..."

"Like a Starwhal?" Coco asked. "They float through space

subsisting on nebula dust and background radiation! I heard some of the scientists talking about them once."

"Are you sure your moon wasn't a Starwhal?" Coco asked, bobbing her head about, giddy with amusement. Her talons danced about on the mesh of the hammock. "Maybe it went away to take a nap in an asteroid belt and didn't get pushed into hyperspace at all!"

"None of that makes sense!" Druthel snapped. He felt his tall ears turn backward, and his face twisted into a snarl. "Nor is it helpful," he said, turning away from the giddy, cheerful little animals, trying too late to hide his unhappiness. The offense he felt at the way they made lighthearted fun of his world's impending destruction was massive. At another time, under different circumstances, their jokes might have been funny. An epic tragedy, however, deserves a measure of solemnity.

Joni took charge of her younger compatriots, pecking each of them in turn on the nape of the neck. She screeched a few words in that pidgin language, and, suddenly, the younger Keats apologized.

"Please keep talking to us," Joni said. "We need to learn more Wrimbrin before we get to Wrombarra. This is why science is for scientists. Language is for Keats. That's the rule we live by, but it's easy to forget. We learn a lot of science, super-ficially, through translating it. Sometimes, younger Keats, forget how small our world on Wespirtech really is and how little we really know."

Druthel's posture relaxed, and his ears straightened out again. These little creatures—somewhere between genius pets and a species in their own right—had clearly meant no harm. And they would be invaluably useful. "True perspective," he said, "is a hard-earned trait. My world has gained a lot of perspective in the wake of the disaster we continue to ride." I hope, he thought, that we survive it. "But, let's not talk about that," he said. "There will be more than enough of that when we get to Wrombarra…"

The planet Wrombarra loomed in front of Druthel's small ship of alien visitors. He'd studied their worlds, and he knew his own planet was smaller, drier, and duller than most the humans chose to inhabit. Instead of emerald continents and sapphire spreads of ocean, dotted with thin webs of white clouds, Wrombarra was covered with swirls of thick gray masses, masking the dusty brown land. Very little of Wrombarra photosynthesized, and none of the wrombarran cities sparkled like diamonds at night, like the cities Druthel had seen shining up from planet Da Vinci. Wrombarrans saw with more of their senses than eyesight, relying a great deal more on sound and vibrations than humans, and they hadn't the same need to light up the night.

Wrombarran civilization stretched in giant nets between ancient magma spires, riddled with caves that had grown in a long passed era on their world. Wrombarran pre-history. Within their recorded history, volcanoes were extremely uncommon on Wrombarra. Until recently…

Druthel's heart ached to see the smears of sulphurous yellow, marring his planet's face above all the newly resurrected volcanoes. There were giant new cracks, visible from space, that rent whole continents, as if an evil creature had raked giant claws across the planet. That creature was gravity, and it was tearing the planet Wrombarra apart from the inside.

As he tore his small ship down through the atmosphere, Druthel saw the bloody red magma spurting and dripping along the face of his world. And, in his mind, he saw the small human scientist, her naked arms wrapped bizarrely around her knees, sitting quietly in the corner of his ship's main hold.

She'd written a paper called, "The Hyper-spatial Quality of Isotopic Variation: An Investigation of the Layers of Hyper-space." He knew she was the key. He would make her work with the other scientists. He would find a way.

The interstellar craft landed in what used to be an empty airfield, many miles from the nearest city. Evacuations had been underway the entire time that Druthel was gone, and whole cities of temporary, tent-like buildings had sprung up in the wilderness. As the grumbling growl of gravity awoke the burning heart of their world, fresh magma had bubbled up from the ground, filling in their cities in the ancient spires, and burning the edges of their net cities, which tore and collapsed, hanging like broken spider webs, dragging unnaturally down to the ground. It did not seem so wise, anymore, to build their homes on the husks of dead volcanoes. Lest those volcanoes arise, zombies intent on mindless killing. If only they'd known. If only they'd been more careful.

Druthel landed the spaceship and then led the human scientists and their three Keats through the tacky, temporary lean-tos of the refugee village to the premier wrombarran science institute. A conglomeration of cutting edge technical building spires, designed to mimic the shape of the giant magma spires that once housed their cities, surrounded the largest acoustiscope dish on the entire planet and an array of smaller echometers. The acoustiscope and echometers were parabolic dishes, shaped and colored like the discarded tips of broken eggshells. Except, they were arranged too neatly, too regularly, and were too massively large to truly be the remnants of eggshells in an abandoned nest.

Druthel walked along the ground through the shanty town beside the field of echometers, instead of flapping his powerful wings and taking to the sky. He wished it were only out of deference for the humans' own incapacity, but, in truth, he was returning to a broken society, spread sadly across the horizontal face of his planet, instead of stretched proudly through the air. A few nets had been strung from the peaks of the spire buildings, but, there hadn't been time for much.

Officials met them; bureaucrats screened them; and assistants guided them, finally to the quarters the humans were being offered. They'd been built a domed insta-concrete building at the base of one of the spires, little more than a hardened tent, but still luxurious compared to what most of the refugees were living in. In addition to basic bedding and a washroom without proper plumbing, the dome contained an ad hoc laboratory, stuffed with computers and other scientific equipment frantically saved from the burning spire city.

"Is this what we're expected to work with?" Einray complained to the group of wrombarran guides watching them. "We should have stayed at Wespirtech," he grumbled. "I can't do anything with this junk."

"Well..." Ivan Bower said, looking at the wrombarrans with their wings folded, "we could try... to..." He clearly wanted to please them but was as deeply troubled as the angry-looking Einray. "No, he's right." Ivan turned to Druthel, the wrombarran he knew best. "This isn't going to work. We need a real laboratory."

Joni was perched on Druthel's shoulder, translating for the room. Druthel said to her, "Tell them this is only their quarters. The equipment here is for them to use, if they want it, but the main laboratories are all in the spire building. When they're settled, I can take them there."

As soon as Joni finished repeating his words, Ivan said, "We're settled. Let's go."

The other humans all agreed, except for Rhiannon who had begun looking through the equipment that had so offended Einray. Druthel and the other wrombarran guides led the rest of the humans to a ground-level entrance to the main spire building, but Rhiannon stayed behind as Druthel feared she would.

Druthel turned to one of the wrombarran aides, a woman he knew well. "Will you guide them?" he said, speaking lowly so Joni would know not to translate. "I need to go back and talk to the human who stayed behind."

"Sure," the aide agreed, flicking her ears lightly.

The rest of the group, including the three Keats, followed the aide into the base of the spire. Druthel turned around, planning to rejoin Rhiannon in the human quarters. Instead, he saw her already leaving.

THE SMALL HUMAN had shed her outer layer of clothing in the wrombarran heat. Now her slender, pink-skinned arms were bare to her shoulders. The shirt she wore scooped loosely at her neck, and her thick mane of hair was pulled back behind her head.

Druthel took his electronic translator out of its waistcoat pocket, clipped it on, and turned it on. "You must be hot," he said.

Rhiannon startled at the sound of his voice, before the translator even began to speak.

Druthel realized his heart was racing and his wings were restless. He should be angry. He'd brought this human many light-years to ascend into the spire and begin work. Instead, she slipped away from the rest of the group and tried to disappear into the refugee city. He didn't have time to look for her if she got lost... Yet, he wasn't sure that anger or impatience were what he was feeling. "Where are you going?" he said.

The small primate woman stared up at Druthel. Wrombarran eyes had no whites, and the dark and light contrast of her eyes captivated him. "I've never been to a planet other than

Da Vinci and its moon, Kong-Fuzi," she said. "Besides... I don't think they'll need me. I told you that back at Wespirtech."

"I think they will," Druthel breathed, almost a reflex. On an impulse, he clicked the tip of his tongue, wanting to feel the shape of Rhiannon with the reflection of that quiet sound. The space she filled in the air in front of him. Wrombarrans used echolocation mostly for navigation while flying, but, it could also be intensely personal. It let him touch her without actually touching her. If another wrombarran had been there... But none was. And Rhiannon didn't know the significance of the quiet click. Nonetheless, Druthel felt embarrassed.

"I'm sorry," Rhiannon said. "I know that you and your people have gone to great expense to bring me here... And, if I thought I could help, I would. But, I think you'll find that the others are much more qualified. They have some interesting theories..."

Rhiannon tilted her head, and Druthel clicked his tongue again, tasting the shape of her subtle gesture. His embarrassment was fading because she was so clearly unbothered. Druthel had always been an awkward man. It was part of why he'd thrown himself into his work. His science. Why did it feel easier to talk to a woman of a different species? A woman he couldn't even understand without an electronic box clipped to his vest?

Rhiannon saw the flickering movement in Druthel's ears. She didn't know what he was thinking, but she knew how important it was to him that her colleagues save his world. So, she kept talking, trying to reassure him that the other Wespirtech scientists were more than competent. "They think they can construct a replacement moon for you. The mass of the outer asteroid belt in your solar system is approximately the same as the mass of your missing moon. So, if we could design a... well... a scoop for a spaceship... like a space tractor..."

Druthel flattened his ears, and Rhiannon's words tripped to a stop. "That won't work," Druthel said.

"You don't want a replacement," Rhiannon said. "You want to reverse the disaster. Bring the original moon back. From hyperspace."

Druthel flared his wings. "Yes," he said. "You understand me." The translated echo of his voice filled his ears with irony, but he didn't care. "All the other strategies—a replacement satellite, counterbalancing the quakes with controlled explosive bursts—they're incomplete. Unstable. We need to reverse the catastrophe... the mistake... when the acoustiscope..." Druthel's enthusiasm drained away as his thoughts drew back to his horrible act of hubris. It hadn't been his act alone.

The whole institute had been devoted to the project for months—using half-phased quark beams to map the topology of local hyperspace. They'd hoped to magnify the power and trace the contours of the cartography of hyperspace much further afield. They'd hoped to develop a map of a deeper layer of hyperspace that would allow them rapid travel—more rapid than human, srellick, or even lintar technology. Instead, the burst of phased quarks had pushed their moon onto a different physical plane. And their home planet quaked with its loss.

As little as a month ago, Druthel had been a vociferous supporter of wrombarran isolation and independence. He'd studied the alien cultures who reigned supreme in their arm of the galaxy, and he knew that small worlds, early in their scientific development, had a way of being consumed by them, only to be regurgitated as tourist planets—dead-ended by the exodus of their greatest minds to join the intellectually exciting, further advanced society of the Human Expansion or the Srellick Mercenary Syndicate.

Druthel hadn't wanted that for his world. He'd hoped that his institute's work on hyperspace cartography would protect his world from ever suffering that fate. It would put them on equal footing. Instead, it had left them crawling, crippled and begging for help.

He should hate this human. This whimsical creature who he knew had the intelligence and insight necessary to help him. But, instead, she sulked and demurred. Yet, all he wanted was to reach out and touch her.

"Take me somewhere on your world," she said. "Show me something—some place—that's special to you." Rhiannon tilted her head and looked up at him. "Your eyes," she said, "they're so dark, I hadn't realized that they're blue."

Druthel blinked and looked away, but the steadiness of her gaze drew him back. Could she be feeling the same strange attraction that he felt for her? It made no sense to him, having feelings like this for another species. But, then, he'd never met another sentient species before... "When we come back," Druthel said, "you'll work?"

Rhiannon nodded her head, swinging the hair gathered in a ponytail behind her head. "Yes, I'll work with you."

Druthel couldn't help thinking that they should already be working with the other scientists in the spire. Yet, the trip here had taken three days. Another few hours wouldn't hurt.

"Come with me," he said, reaching out a winged arm. His furry fingers at the hinged joint of his wing wrapped around Rhiannon's bare-skinned fingers. Her skin was smooth like the skin of his wings, just like his sonar had told him it would be. "Where we're going," he said, "I'll have to fly, so wrap your arms around me." He guided her around his back, where she grasped his neck with her thin, flightless arms. "You should be light enough to carry."

As soon as his wings began to beat, Druthel started clicking his tongue in a rhythm. He felt the shape of the empty air in front of him, and he pulled them both through it, ascending to the sky. Once they were high enough above the makeshift city, drawing further and further away from the artificial spire housing the other scientists and all their work and equipment, Druthel relaxed his wings into a glide. Air cut above and below him, but he caught the wind of a powerful current. His body felt out of balance and heavy with Rhiannon clinging to his back, so he tilted his shoulders forward to compensate.

He marveled as they flew together that Rhiannon had willingly put herself in such a dangerous situation—many meters above the ground—for a flightless creature. He couldn't help but feel a rush at the power it gave him over her, but he also felt himself intrigued by her trust. And drawn to protect this helpless creature that was a silent, warm weight upon his back.

For her part, Rhiannon buried her face deep in the fur on Druthel's neck. The whistling rush of air around her was exhilarating but also terrifying. But, then, so was the feel of his fur against her arms and face.

When she risked looking out over his shoulder again, Rhiannon saw that Druthel was flying them toward a canyon. The base of the gorge was a pool of bright colors, all pink, chartreuse, and neon. Alien plant life? Rhiannon wondered, but Druthel turned swiftly about before she could get a good look at it. She buried her face in his fur again.

"We've landed," Druthel said, his translator echoing his words in Solanese. "You can let go."

It took Rhiannon another moment to trust the sensation of being stationary again. She relaxed her hold on Druthel's shoulders tentatively. She didn't let go entirely until he hunched down low enough for her feet to firmly touch the ground.

Druthel watched Rhiannon as she looked out from the cave in the cliff face of the canyon that they'd landed in. It was a mere pocket in the rock, big enough to hold the two of them but not much more. Druthel thought it might have been a large bubble in the magma when this igneous rock had formed millions of years ago. Since then, the chemotrophic lifeforms—analogues to the photosynthetic lifeforms on most human worlds—had eaten their way down through the rock, revealing the underground bubbles beneath.

Although Rhiannon's specialty was quantum chemistry, she had been exposed to enough biology to make a solid guess as to what she was looking at. "Those plumes of color in the pools down there..." she said, "...that's chemotrophic life?" She wasn't sure if the translator would know scientific words like that. But it did.

"Yes," Druthel said. "The bacto-bogs are the building blocks of life on my planet. They convert heat in the spring water and iron from the rocks into energy. Then the swarmers eat the bactoforms; avians eat the swarmers; and we eat avians. The chain of life."

Rhiannon cocked an eyebrow, that thin semi-circle of fur. "Your species is carnivorous, then?"

"Right."

"And you eat birds..."

Druthel saw immediately where she was heading. "The Keats are safe. They are so different from our own avians—anyone can see in an instant that they're alien. It would be dangerous to eat them. It might insult their owners—"

"It would insult their owners," Rhiannon interrupted.

"—and their bright plumage might even mean they're poisonous. But, yes, I did think they might have been brought on board as snacks."

"That must have offended them," Rhiannon said, lowering herself to the floor of the cave. She sat down and leaned her back against the cave wall.

"Apparently the words for pet and snack are very different in Solanese," Druthel said. He folded his knees up, trying to sit down beside Rhiannon. He simply wasn't built for it, and his wings crushed uncomfortably against the ground. "They're essentially the same word in Wrimbrin."

Rhiannon laughed.

"Fortunately, my electronic translator happened to pick the less offensive option until I figured out what was going on." Druthel shifted his wings and accidentally hit Rhiannon in the shoulder.

"Here," she said, taking the edge of his wing—his thickly muscled arm—in her hand. She helped him stretch out and refold the wing less awkwardly. In the process, his arm ended up around her, draped over her back.

"Thank you," he said.

"Why do you come here if it's so uncomfortable for you?"

Druthel pointed up with one of the fingers at the joint of his other wing. Rhiannon looked up and saw a metal bar installed in the ceiling.

"Usually, I hang upside down," Druthel said.

"I don't mean to stop you..." Rhiannon said, starting to shift her body under the light pressure of his leathery wing as if she meant to stand up.

"No, that's okay," Druthel said. He liked the feel of Rhiannon close to him. "If you don't mind my wing over you, this configuration works for me."

Rhiannon didn't answer, so Druthel assumed she must be okay. They sat together, staring out at the bacto-bogs. Fist-sized swarmers with glittery exoskeletons flitted about above the pools. Sunlight glinted off the swarms as they flew in formation, first one way then the other. Their aimless flight patterns were soothing to watch. It's why Druthel liked coming there.

"This is peaceful," he said. Though, as he said it, he felt the rumble of a minor quake in the stone around them. He knew the quakes were much worse at the city spires, and the gentle rumble he felt here could be shaking homes and property to rubble farther away. While his people cowered in a makeshift city in the desert, he was secluded with a member of an alien race so far advanced that the fate of a single world seemed small to them.

"I'm going to tell you why I don't want to work with you," Rhiannon said.

Druthel's wings constricted, pressing against her, for her words filled him with anger. But, she continued to speak as the translator echoed her, so Druthel forced himself to be calm and listen.

"The last project I worked on was an algae pack air convertor," she said. "Highly compact. Highly efficient. It's so much better than the current state of the art that every station and spaceship in the Expansion will fork over the money to have their systems upgraded before the year's over."

"That's... good?" Druthel said. They were both still staring out of the cave at the lazily drifting colors of the bacto-bog, but Druthel could feel bitter laughter shake Rhiannon's body.

"You'd think that, wouldn't you?"

The voice of the translator stayed the same, but Druthel could hear a change in Rhiannon's tone. She sounded sad and a little angry.

"My roommate and I developed them," she said. "I don't usually work on projects with so much biology, but Keida's a biologist, and, well, the idea just kind of came together. One night we were lying in our room in the dark, talking across the space between our beds about how Einray was collaborating with a biologist to grow chrono-accelerated trees, and the next thing we knew, we'd come up with our own bizarre bio-physics collaboration."

Druthel remembered the empty bed in Rhiannon's room. "Your roommate left Wespirtech?" he asked.

"Yes," Rhiannon said. "She found out that the algae we gengineered for the air convertors releases a low level toxin. It's nothing really... It can be filtered out. Though, the filters do take up more space than the original algae packs... and they'd need to be scrubbed every few months..."

Rhiannon trailed off, and the two of them sat in silence until another tremor shook their cave. Druthel shifted his weight restlessly. "If it's nothing," he said, "why did she leave?"

Rhiannon's voice was very quiet when she spoke, but the translator managed to pick it up: "Most people aren't allergic to the toxin. In fact... We haven't found any humans who are. The only people allergic to it that we've found are members of a species called Hoilyn. Some of them work at Wespirtech. In low level jobs. They're not powerful. No one will listen to them. No one will install the filters just for them."

"So don't publish your research," Druthel said.

"Too late." Rhiannon laughed again. It was a sad laugh. "We didn't realize the problem until the algae packs were installed in Wespirtech. Hoilyn workers and some of their children went into anaphylactic shock. We got them shipped down to Da Vinci in respirators—the ones we got to in time—but, once these algae packs are installed everywhere, we've essentially cut their species off from space. Me and Keida, single-handedly."

"So you work to fix it!" Druthel declared.

Rhiannon's head lowered. "That's not my area," Rhiannon said. "I did the chemistry, designing the catalyzation process in the algae chloroplasts. Keida's the one who understands the biology. And she's gone off to be a doctor in the asteroid belt of Hegula Hephasta. Somewhere she can do some real good." The final words were ones Keida had said to Rhiannon the last time they'd seen each other. They still stung.

"Then she's a coward," Druthel said simply. "A scientist doesn't abandon research entirely because she's made... a mistake." The translated word hung in the air between them. A horrible, horrific understatement when sitting on a world that once again rumbled with the symptoms of the wrombarrans' own mistake. A mistake that Druthel had played a part in.

He understood the impulse that Rhiannon's roommate felt: leave research behind and find a simple, straightforward way to do good. But that didn't make it right. "I hope you're not planning to follow your roommate's example," Druthel said. Though, they both knew she was. Rhiannon's behavior had made that abundantly apparent. "But, if you are, then I have to remind you of your promise: I brought you somewhere special to me. Now you must work with me to save my world."

"Yes, I'll help."

Druthel couldn't help feeling a measure of sympathy for the small human huddled under his wing. They had more in common than he would have thought. More than their disparate biologies and electronically translated languages would suggest. "Let's go back, then," he said, and Rhiannon meekly complied.

BACK IN THE LAB, Rhiannon became a different person. No longer the scared, uncertain creature that had huddled under Druthel's wing, whispering grave confessions, she stood tall. As tall as her stature, barely half Druthel's height, let her. And she spoke with confidence.

The flurry of voices—human, Keat, wrombarran, srellick, and electronic—made it hard for Druthel to keep up with any particular individual's contributions. It was more a question of following the zeitgeist of any particular line of research. Geologists shouted out ideas for stabilizing fault lines on Wrombarra's populated continents. Physicists exclaimed discoveries about how to tune the array of echometers. And in the middle of it all, Rhiannon was the spark of insight and inspiration that Druthel hoped she would be. He was in awe of her. His instincts about her had been right, and he took pride in every contribution she made, if only for his small part in bringing her here.

She didn't speak often. And, when she did, Druthel often missed the exact words, for she spoke quietly and with brevity. Only a few words. Yet, the storm of ideas would morph around her. The other humans would grow quieter for a moment, tilt their heads, stand a little straighter. Subtle changes. Then the cacophony of voices would start again, and it was all Druthel could do to follow in the wake of the wave.

Joni, Lulu, and Coco were in high demand, flying from shoulder to shoulder, trying to translate where ever they could be most useful.

The storm of ideas lasted from morning until late at night, for days on end. Scant time was taken for hastily rushed meals. And all the while, quakes grew more powerful, ushering the scientists to work harder, concentrate more fiercely. Find the solution.

While the team of geologists focused on stabilizing Wrombarra without a moon and a splinter group continued to work on methods of constructing a replacement moon out of asteroids, the bulk of the physicists followed Druthel and Rhiannon's lead. Probes were constructed that could send carefully modulated signals back through hyperspace, and a series of them—each larger than the last—was sent across the threshold between normal space and hyperspace, chasing after the moon, ever deeper into that parallel dimension. The automated signals sent back data that proved unequivocally several things.

First, although Wrombarra was no longer affected by the gravitational pull of its moon, the moon continued to be affected by the gravity of Wrombarra. It was still orbiting, only in a different dimension. Gravity passed into hyperspace but not out, like light through a one-way mirror. Second, the solar radiation from Wrombarra's sun passed into hyperspace just as gravity did. So, even in the depths of hyperspace, Wrombarra's moon was still touched with sunlight. And, finally, the massier the object sent into hyperspace, the greater the energy necessary to bring it back. So, while a spaceship could skip in and out of hyperspace, barely skimming the surface, an object as large as Wrombarra's moon would have fallen to an almost impossible depth once breaching the barrier between hyper- and normal space. It would be almost impossible to bring back.

Druthel stared at the lines of numbers that streamed across the computer terminal. The data from the probes continued to stream back to them from hyperspace, but it was not heartening. Druthel could sense the tone in the room. The fragments of speech he caught through the electronic translator or through Joni's announcements told him that the human and srellick members of his team were giving up. Most of his own colleagues, the other wrombarrans, had moved on, days ago, to helping the geologists or the splinter sect working with asteroids.

They were more scared of failing to stop the quakes than they were driven to succeed. Fear of failure made them short-sighted. Though, in this case, their choice might prove right: it would take the energy of a supernova, perhaps several, to bring their moon back. If he'd stopped chasing this dead end days ago, perhaps he could have sped up the work on building an artificial moon. He could have saved precious days. And saving days could save lives...

Then, in the midst of his despair and self-recrimination, Druthel heard Rhiannon speak. Her voice was soft but clear to him in the crowd of voices. He always listened for her voice carefully. Usually, the others—especially her own human colleagues—did too. This time, Einray laughed, and Karlingoff spoke chidingly. The conversation didn't halt for her. Joni didn't bother to translate, and Druthel couldn't make out Rhiannon's words from the jumble of electronic translation.

"Wait," he said, looking up from the computer and seeking out Rhiannon's gaze. "What did you say?" he said to her, but she stared back at him uncomprehendingly. Druthel turned to Joni: "What did Rhiannon say?" he asked. "Tell her to repeat it."

Joni passed on the message, and then she passed back Rhiannon's response: "She said, If we can't bring the moon back, maybe we could drop Wrombarra into hyperspace with it."

Druthel folded his wing, bringing the hand at the joint to his muzzle. His eyes were locked on Rhiannon's, and he'd grown accustomed enough to her body language to tell that she was scared. He could see her hands shaking. She spoke in a whisper, but he had no way to translate the words. Everyone else in the lab was shouting, and even the Keats had got swept up in the heat of the argument themselves, breaking into and out of their pidgin language.

The only side of the argument that Druthel could understand was wrombarran, and there was no consensus from them. Half the scientists loved Rhiannon's idea. The others were furious: "Wrombarra will be cut off from the rest of galactic society!" one of his colleagues cried. Another shouted back, "Who cares? We were isolated to begin with!" The argument raged on, and the only thing clear was that Rhiannon's idea had taken on a life of its own.

Within the hour, calculations were completed for the exact power and frequency of an acoustiscope beam to push Wrombarra through the fabric of space, breaching the barrier into hyperspace. The planet's own mass would carry it downward—metaphorically speaking—from there. It would settle to an appropriate depth, and then it would continue to orbit the sun as if nothing had changed, except for regaining its moon.

The only difference would be that no spaceship from Wrombarra would ever be able to muster the energy to escape from that depth of hyperspace. All of wrombarran society would be cut off from the rest of normal space. Forever.

The tone in the lab had utterly shifted. Instead of three separate groups competing to cure Wrombarra's lunar cavity as fast as possible, now there were only two groups. A handful of scientists jubilantly worked on the design for a shipboard acoustiscope that the srellick ship could carry into space and aim at Wrombarra. Everyone else watched them in hushed disquietude.

Before the sect of scientists who wanted to sink Wrombarra into hyperspace could finish their designs, a delegation from the high government arrived. Someone must have slipped out of the lab and informed them.

All the scientists were sent home. Forcibly in a few cases. Quietly in most. The question of whether to sink Wrombarra into hyperspace had become a government matter, and the government didn't want research continued that could lead to an irreversible situation. At least, not until the representative council voted on it.

DRUTHEL DIDN'T KNOW what to do with himself outside of the lab. His brain was buzzing, torn between elation at his triumph, shock at the twist their research had taken, and despair at the finality of their discovery. He had been right! Rhiannon was the key. And his planet was savable.

But the cost... It was one thing to spurn the society of the rest of the galaxy. It was another to be cut off from it forever.

Druthel found Rhiannon at the base of the spire, outside the human quarters and alone. He hadn't realized he was looking for her, merely turning restless circles in the sky, until he found her. She'd disappeared from the lab so quickly when the officials came...

Druthel landed a few feet from Rhiannon. She was sitting on the ground with her arms wrapped around her knees in much the pose she'd been in when he first laid eyes on her.

"You did it," he said.

She turned her face and looked up at him as the translator spoke to her. "Yes," she said, in response. "I've cut another species off from space travel."

"Is that so bad?" Druthel asked. "Besides, we won't know that until we know what the council decides."

"Well, then, maybe I haven't done it," Rhiannon said. "Either way... I don't see how to be happy about this." Rhiannon's mouth turned down in a sad expression.

Druthel didn't know how to cheer her. He understood feeling conflicted about this triumph. Yet, it was a triumph. Wasn't it? "Fly with me again," he said.

"Okay," Rhiannon said, pushing herself up from the ground. "Take me somewhere new. Show me something I haven't seen." She didn't say, something I won't have the chance to see again.

Rhiannon climbed aboard Druthel's broad back and wrapped her arms around his neck. She kept her eyes open this flight, despite the fear in the pit of her stomach. She couldn't miss these sights. She'd never forgive herself once they were gone.

Druthel flew away from the bacto-bogs. He flew toward the city he'd lived in most of his life. The towering magma spire that had recently been a bustling city, thick with wrombarrans in flight. Now the air was empty, except for gusts of heat that singed his wings. He'd never seen the city devoid of wrombarrans circling it at every height.

It was a desolate cone of cinder and molten rock now. Red twisted down its sides, dripping hideously out of the caves that had once been entrances to the caverns and tunnels—his people's homes—inside. Those would be gone now. Filled with new, molten rock. It would take his people forever to rebuild, even if their planet's core settled down. Everything that hadn't been brought with them to the refugee camps would be gone. From what news Druthel had heard, all the other major cities were the same.

Druthel circled the city, closer and closer, until he could take the heat no more. With a swoop to a higher, cooler current, Druthel abandoned the city. Rhiannon clung tightly to his neck, and he realized that he'd exposed her unprotected skin, bare of fur, to the same heat that he could hardly withstand. He was sorry, but he took a grim satisfaction in it too. She acted like a scapegoat, blaming herself for his world's self-begotten misfortune. And he badly needed a scapegoat right then.

Druthel flew back to the shanty town, but a squeeze on his neck made him think that maybe Rhiannon didn't want to go back yet either. So, instead of stopping, he flew on, bringing them back to the small cave overlooking the bacto-bog.

This time, after Rhiannon climbed down from his back, Druthel put all his weight on his arms and lifted his feet up into the air. He grabbed the metal bar in the ceiling and hung comfortably above Rhiannon who'd curled up in her knee-hugging pose. Their heads were close, only inches apart.

"Is your skin okay?" he asked.

Rhiannon looked flushed; a pink glow suffused her face and arms, but she said, "I'm fine." It felt like a sunburn, but she didn't mind. "How long will it take?" she asked. "For your government to decide."

Druthel didn't know, but he imagined they would decide quickly. Every day, the world was worse off. There was no incentive to wait. "If they decide quickly," he said, "then your team will be leaving. It won't take long to build that acoustis-cope. In fact, I know they sent everyone home... but I'd be surprised if there wasn't a functional design finished tonight."

Druthel had been a staunch supporter of wrombarran

isolation. Now he could have his wish, but it wasn't his wish any more.

"I've enjoyed working with you," he said.

Rhiannon was quiet for a long time. Then, she said, "I'm sorry I couldn't fix it better."

"At least you fixed it," he said.

There were no more words shared that night, but, in the gentle glowing light from the bacto-forms, Rhiannon turned her face towards Druthel's. Her mane brushed his muzzle, and he clicked his tongue to feel the shape of her alien body with his sonar. So close beside him. A moment later, she reached her hand towards his, and he found his fingers clasping hers. She stood up, moving her body, upside down compared to his, toward him. But she was small, and a slight pressure from his wing somersaulted her against him. He helped her hook her feet into the bar beside his own, and then he wrapped his wings around her.

They slept together, hanging in his cave, overlooking the bacto-bogs until morning.

THE GLOW of the sun illuminated the orangey-hue of the bacto-bogs like fire. Unlike the magma, though, their light was life and giving.

Druthel and Rhiannon awoke groggy and confused. They flew back together in a silence less comfortable than the one they'd shared all night. Druthel was confused by his feelings for Rhiannon. All these years, he'd hated humans—an abstract concept, a species of conquerors. But if he had the freedom, he would have flown this one small human all over his world, showing her everything that made it beautiful. He would have followed her back to her own lunar home on Wespirtech, merely hoping to learn more about her.

This alien woman's brilliance had set the wheels in motion that Druthel believed would save his planet. Her enigmatic brilliance that she herself felt guilty for... He wanted to show her that she had nothing to regret. Yet, if her plan was approved, he would barely have time to say goodbye.

Druthel and Rhiannon went straight to the lab and found it already filled and buzzing. Despite the government order to halt work, several of Druthel's wrombarran colleagues had continued to work through the night. Much as Druthel expected. They'd finished the designs for a shipboard acoustiscope and built a haphazard, ramshackle prototype of the two meter wide dish. The srellick scientists were already outside, wiring it to their ship and cementing it to the hull.

"Where were you?" one of his colleagues asked Druthel. "You missed out on building the device that will save our world!"

Druthel looked at Rhiannon, but he didn't answer. His wrombarran colleague didn't really want an answer and was already regaling him with bleary-eyed boasts about the sleepless night of work.

"I guess, you didn't feel like you needed any extra glory?" the colleague asked, rhetorically again. "You brought us the scientist who came up with the idea!" Druthel's colleague folded his wings in an elaborate bow before Rhiannon. Within moments, every wrombarran in the room followed suit, and soon the humans joined in with their own custom, clapping their hands together in a cacophony of applause.

"You will be remembered as a goddess here," a wrombarran woman told Rhiannon. Joni translated.

Other wrombarrans spoke up, thanking Rhiannon, congratulating her, and promising she'd be remembered forever in the depths of hyperspace. A mythical wise woman. A warrior of science. A few of Druthel's wrombarran colleagues kept quiet —individuals who he knew had wanted to end the isolation of their planet. They would remember her always as a hellish jailer who locked their planet up and threw away the key. Thankfully, they were tactful enough to hold their tongues.

Druthel, however, knew that he'd always remember Rhiannon as the scared little girl, hiding under his wing. As the woman who held him through the longest night of his life. He realized wistfully that if the situation were different, he might be able to fall in love with her.

Before long, a delegate from the government council arrived. As all the wrombarrans expected, their government had indeed come to a conclusion overnight: time was of the essence, and isolation was not a significant concern. Since the acoustiscope was ready—the srellicks had finished attaching it —the alien scientists would leave at sundown. The srellicks could take the humans home. And Wrombar would be pushed through the barrier into hyperspace before the sun rose tomorrow.

"This is so fast..." Rhiannon said. If she hadn't been standing right beside Druthel, his translator wouldn't have picked it up. He'd turned the sensitivity down so that it wouldn't flood him with the words of every human in the room.

"There's no reason to wait," he said. "Except for us." He looked at her softly. "But that's not a reason." He traced a finger along the curve of Rhiannon's triangular jaw. He clicked his tongue and felt the smooth, flat shape of her face with sonar. Then he lowered his own face to her height and nuzzled her softly with his furry muzzle. "Thank you for saving my world."

He felt her smile against his fur. She whispered in his ear, and a moment later the electronic voice translated for him, "Explore hyperspace for me, okay?" Her alien voice was soft and melodic in his ear. "Maybe there's something amazing down there. Something much more interesting than in normal space. If not... well, there will be soon."

Druthel wrapped his wings around her, pressing her small

body against him again. The embrace was brief. They were already getting looks from the other scientists in the room. As he pulled away from her, though, Druthel said, "Promise me that you won't stop researching. You can do too much good."

Rhiannon smiled thinly. She didn't promise, but she did nod.

The rest of the day passed in a flash. The refugees in the shanty town pulled all their resources together and celebrated the impending launch of the srellick vessel with a parade. Wrombarrans, dressed in colorful flowing ribbons, flew across the sky in cartwheeling, crisscrossing chains. They showered the on-looking alien dignitaries in fallen feathers, a soft down gathered from native avians. Everyone feasted at a spontaneous pot-luck party held around the srellick vessel.

Then, as the sun set, Druthel watched with his people as the srellick and humans, his own Rhiannon included, filed onto the srellick vessel. She turned as she entered the hatch and looked over the crowd until she saw Druthel. She waved her delicate, wingless hand. Then, she turned again and was gone. The hatch closed behind the last of them, and the crowd waited, impatient and restless, for the engines to start.

As they waited, the wrombarrans began to sing, a folk song that even wrombarran children knew. Their voices trilled together, rising in harmony, until the field was filled with their song. The sound of srellick engines starting drowned out the singing, and the wrombarran voices morphed into an inarticulate cheer.

Druthel watched the vessel rise into the sky on a trail of white smoke. It dwindled to the pinpoint of a falling star, and then it disappeared altogether. The darkness of the night altered, however, and Druthel turned to see his planet's moon shining behind him.

∾

On a spaceship many layers of hyperspace away, Rhiannon watched the pale dun disk of Wrombarra wink out of existence as eerily as its moon had months ago. She could still remember the warm feeling of Druthel's leathery wings wrapped around her, and the promise he'd asked of her echoed in her ears.

Rhiannon wasn't comfortable with the solution her science had found for his people, but his people had seemed happy with it. Perhaps, she could find a similar solution for the last race she'd locked away from her own society. Rhiannon decided she'd send a message to Keida when she got back to Wespirtech. She'd need help if she was going to design portable, personal air filters for the Hoilyn. It wasn't a perfect solution. But it would be better.

ABOUT THE AUTHOR

Mary E. Lowd is a prolific science-fiction and furry writer in Oregon. She's had more than 200 short stories and a dozen novels published, always with more on the way. Her work has won three Ursa Major Awards, ten Leo Literary Awards, and four Cóyotl Awards. She edited FurPlanet's ROAR anthology series for five years, and she is now the editor and founder of the furry e-zine *Zooscape*. She lives in a crashed spaceship, disguised as a house and hidden behind a rose garden, with an extensive menagerie of animals, some real and some imaginary.

For more information:
marylowd.com

To read Mary's short stories:
deepskyanchor.com

ALSO BY MARY E. LOWD

Otters in Space

Otters In Space

Otters In Space 2: Jupiter, Deadly

Otters In Space 3: Octopus Ascending

The Celestial Fragments (A Labyrinth of Souls Trilogy)

The Snake's Song

The Bee's Waltz

The Otter's Wings

The Entangled Universe

Entanglement Bound

The Entropy Fountain

Starwhal in Flight

Xeno-Spectre

Hell Moon

The Ancient Egg

In a Dog's World

Jove Deadly's Lunar Detective Agency

The Necromouser and Other Magical Cats

You're Cordially Invited to Crossroads Station

Queen Hazel and Beloved Beverly

Tri-Galactic Trek

Nexus Nine

Some Words Burn Brightly: An Illuminated Collection of Poetry